SECRET OF THE DRAGON

A DRAGON FANTASY ADVENTURE

JASMINE WALT

DYNAMO PRESS

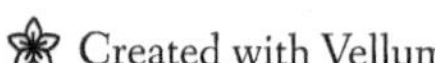 Created with Vellum

ONE

"*Zara. It's time to wake up.*"

A low, feminine voice wound its way through my dreams, tugging me awake. At first I resisted, drifting through the darkness, allowing my body to float in the peaceful nothingness that had become my life. My body felt heavy. Lethargic. Certainly incapable of motion. I could sleep for another month. Maybe even a year.

"*Zara.*"

That voice again. Wait. Why was there a voice speaking in my head? The only mental voice I ever heard aside from my own was—

"Lessie!"

My eyes flew open, my heart pounding with fear and anxiety. A sloped ceiling made of wooden slats greeted me, along with twittering birds and sunlight streaming in through open windows. I was lying on the floor of some cabin or hut, no more than ten-by-ten feet. The thick, ropey branches of some kind of tropical tree waved at me from outside the window. Where the hell was I? The last thing I remembered was...

"Lessie?" I called through the bond. That's right—my last memory was of the two of us collapsing on an unknown island after Muza had helped us escape the Hellmouth. I'd traveled to the Underworld, convinced the death god to destroy a piece of the dragon god's heart, and had nearly fallen to my death trying to make it out. Lessie had saved me, but in the process, had inhaled a terrifying amount of the poisonous gas that swirled around the mountain. When the two of us had passed out, I thought we were dying. But now...

"Lessie?" I tried again, growing more anxious by the second. I could feel her through the bond, very faintly, but had no idea where she was. Had we been separated somehow? I tried to stand up so I could look out the window, but the effort of sitting up alone made me dizzy. Panting, I lay back down on the floor, trying to get my breath back.

"Good. You are awake." That voice again! *"Stay right there. Muza is coming to help you."*

"Who are you?" I demanded, puzzled and exasperated. Were there other humans or creatures capable of mind-speech? *"And how do you know Muza?"*

"I will explain later," the voice said firmly. *"For now, you need sustenance."*

The sound of flapping wings distracted me from the voice. Groaning, I reached for the windowsill and used it to pull myself to my feet. I was still wearing the same clothes, grimy from who knew how many days of travel. When was the last time I'd bathed? Or eaten? How long had I been out?

Muza pulled up alongside my window, chuffing impatiently. His silver scales shimmered brightly in the sun, nearly blinding me with their luminescence. The sight of him calmed me—he was Tavarian's dragon, and the fact that he was still alive meant that Tavarian was, too.

"What do you want from me?" I asked, leaning out the window to look at Muza. I swallowed hard when I saw how high up we were—I seemed to be in some kind of treehouse. Muza had his left wing extended, forming a sort of bridge, which under normal circumstances I could use to climb onto his back. "In case you haven't noticed, I have the grace of an eel on dry land right now. There's no way I can climb on your back."

Muza rolled his eyes, pulling away. He flapped his wings, pummeling me with a gust of wind. For a second I thought he was flying away, but then his clawed arm shot through the window. Taloned fingers wrapped around my torso, and I shrieked in surprise as he dragged me outside.

"Hey!" I cried.

The giant dragon, who was easily four times the size of the tree house I'd been convalescing in, soared away. My heart raced as I dangled from his claws—I wasn't used to traveling this way, as if I were prey. Strange trees with blue and purple leaves flitted past us, and beyond, the ocean sparkled in an endless wave of sun-kissed aquamarine.

Muza gently deposited me next to a spring tucked in the middle of the forest. I lunged toward the clear water almost before I hit the ground, achingly aware of how parched my throat was. Cool, sweet water flowed over my tongue, and I gulped it down until my stomach cramped and I was forced to roll onto my back, panting with the effort. Dragon's balls, I was as weak as a kitten! What happened to me? And how was I still alive?

A large shape loomed over me, and for a minute I thought it was Muza. But when I blinked the water out of my eyes, the shape came into focus, and I realized this dragon wasn't Muza at all. He was bronze, with golden spikes and green eyes that glittered like gemstones in his broad face.

"*Hello,*" he said, his voice as clear as a bell in my head.

"Y-you talked! In my head!" Adrenaline kicked in, and I scrambled backward through the mud. "T-that's not possible!" Dragons could communicate via mindspeech, but only with each other and their bonded rider. No rider had ever been able to directly communicate with another rider's dragon.

"*I am not another rider's dragon,*" the dragon said, drawing himself upright. He spread his wings wide, and my breath caught at the striking, formidable figure he made, backlit by the blazing sun. "*My name is Serpol, and I am a free dragon.*"

"A free dragon?" I stared. "*What the hell does that mean?*"

Muza interrupted our chat by landing next to me with a heavy thud. He offered me the large branch in his claws, which was laden with round, orange fruits roughly the size of my head.

"*Eat,*" Serpol urged. "*The fruit will help you regain your strength.*"

After a moment's hesitation, I plucked one of the fruits off the branch. I dipped it in the spring to clean off the dirt, then I took a bite. It was firm but juicy, and I groaned a little at the explosion of honeyed sweetness in my mouth. The instant sugar rush made me forget the weakness in my limbs and the fuzziness in my head, and I chowed down with a single-minded intensity.

"*Much better,*" the dragon said approvingly as I annihilated a second piece of fruit. "*You have color in your cheeks again, which Muza informs me is a good sign in humans.*"

I glanced up at him. "Have you ever seen a human before?"

"*Only Muza's rider, when he brought him here the first time.*" Those gemlike eyes sparkled with what I was beginning to realize was fascination. "*You are so small. I can't understand how your kind was ever able to subdue ours.*"

"There was magic involved," I said in a wry voice, tossing the pit aside. "So by 'free dragon,' do you mean that you're not bonded to a rider, then? How is that possible? I thought Akron the Defender and his army of mages subdued all the dragons. That's how we were able to defeat the dragon god." By capturing his dragons and forcing them into bonded slavery, the Dragon War mages had weakened Zakyiar to the point that they were able to defeat him in battle.

"*A handful of us managed to escape when Zakyiar was at his weakest point, and nobody noticed,*" Serpol said proudly. "*My ancestors flew many miles east, and then south, before we eventually settled on this archipelago. We have been living here for thousands of years.*"

Thousands of years. I looked at Muza, and the truth was right there in his eyes. "So this is where you've been living all along," I murmured, reaching out to run a hand along his silver snout. "You've been hiding out here the whole time, haven't you?"

Muza nodded his head.

"Just how many of you live here?" I asked, turning back to Serpol. "How far away are we from Elantia? Do you only live here, or—"

"*It is better to show you rather than tell,*" Serpol said. "*But first, I highly recommend you take advantage of the spring and wash.*" His snout twitched, as if he were wrinkling his nose, and I blushed. "*You'll want to smell better than that when I take you to Lessie.*"

"Lessie!" In all the confusion and excitement, I'd completely forgotten about her. "How is she? Is she on the island? She wouldn't answer when I called, and—"

"*Bath,*" Serpol said sternly. He plucked me from the ground, then dumped me unceremoniously into the water, clothes and all. Sputtering, I came up for air, ready to give him a piece of my mind, but Serpol and Muza were already lumbering away, their great spiked tails swishing through the grass.

"*We will give you some privacy so you can bathe properly. Try not to get into any trouble.*"

The dragons launched themselves into the sky, and I resisted the urge to stick out my tongue at them. Clambering out of the water, I stripped off my clothes, squeezed out the excess water, then laid them out on a small boulder to dry. If Tavarian were here, he could dry them with his magic, but since he wasn't, I'd just have to make do with what nature had to offer.

A pang of longing struck my heart at the thought of my fiancé, and I brushed a thumb over the ring on my finger. It was still a little weird to think of him as my betrothed, especially considering the circumstances under which we'd met, but there was no denying that I loved him fiercely and wanted to spend the rest of my life with him. I wondered if he was still in Warosia, negotiating our alliance, or if he'd returned to Polyba by now. Rhia and Halldor would have made it back by now—what were they telling the others? That Lessie and I hadn't made it? The idea that Tavarian thought me dead made my heart ache. Hopefully, Muza would get him a message soon telling him that we were okay.

Despite my annoyance with Serpol for throwing me into the water, I was happy to go back in and wash the grime off. Dunking my head beneath the surface, I scrubbed my hair clean as best as I could. The water here was crystal clear, and I could see patches of strange, colorful plants waving lazily a few feet away. Fish darted between the rainbow leaves, their blue and orange scales sparkling.

When I couldn't hold my breath any longer, I lifted my head from the water, then slicked my hair away from my face and floated on my back. As I stared up at the cloudless blue sky, waiting for the dragons to return, I basked in the peacefulness of this place. There was a quietness to the air I wasn't used to, even though I'd spent much of my life in the wilderness. This place was a true sanctuary, and aside from Tavarian's treehouse—or at least I assumed it was his, since he was the only one who knew this place—it was untouched by human hands.

I was just drifting off to sleep when a rumbling sound caught my attention. Opening an eye, I glanced toward the tree line just in time to see a giant, boar-like creature with bright yellow fur burst into the clearing. Its orange eyes rolled madly in its head as it barreled toward me, huge golden tusks glinting in the morning light, dust kicking up in a cloud around it.

"Dragon's balls!" I yelped, jumping out of the water. The boar charged straight into the pond, narrowly missing me.

Pumping my limbs as fast as they would go, I raced for the nearest tree and scrambled up it, ignoring the way the rough bark scraped at my bare skin. Leaves and branches pricked at my arms and legs as I wrapped myself around one of the tree's thicker limbs and held on for dear life.

The boar was not impressed with my attempt to get away. It ran up to the tree, then snorted and pawed at the ground before rearing up on its hind legs. One of its tusks sliced the side of my leg, and I squealed as I jerked my injured limb away.

Dammit! I was bleeding. It was only a matter of time before I attracted other predators. I wished I'd grabbed my weapons, but they were still by the pond. And I couldn't climb much higher than this—the branches above me were spindly and didn't look up to supporting my weight.

I was just considering the idea of leaping to the next tree when an ear-splitting roar shook the air. Lessie dove from the sky, her maw open wide. She snatched up the boar in her vast jaws before it could react and raced off to the edge of the pond with it. The sickening crunch of bone as she crushed the animal in her maw made me cringe, and the boar's death knell rang out briefly before everything went silent.

"I can't leave you alone for a few minutes, can I?" Lessie complained. She dropped the mangled boar carcass and ambled over to the tree. *"I suppose Serpol wouldn't understand how*

fragile humans are, but Muza should have known better than to leave you out here defenseless."

"I'm not defenseless," I grumbled as she plucked me out of the tree. The scales on the inside of her paw were warm and smooth against my skin, and I allowed her to cradle me for a minute before setting me down. "I can fight."

Lessie snorted. "*Yes, when you don't leave your weapons by the pond.*" But she nuzzled me, and affection washed over me through the bond. "*I'm glad you're safe, either way.*"

"You too." I leaned my head against her cheek, careful to avoid her crown of spikes. "I thought we were dead, Lessie."

"*We almost were. If Yalora hadn't used her magic to save us, we would have gone straight to the death god's realm.*"

I shuddered. "Yeah, no thanks." I'd *just* escaped from there and had no desire to go back any time soon. "Who is Yalora?"

"*Serpol's mother,*" Lessie explained. "*He comes from a long line of dragon mages.*"

"Dragon mages?" I gaped. "As in, dragons who can do magic?"

"*Well, what else is it supposed to mean?*" Lessie teased as she rolled onto her back. "*You'd better bring your clothes over here so I can get them dry. This is no place for humans to run around naked.*"

I went to get my clothes from the boulder they were drying on, my head still reeling from the implications. I'd never heard of dragons being able to do magic before. And these dragons could freely speak to any human, and weren't bonded. What else could they do? How many were on the island? What other secrets did this place hold?

I brought my clothes over to Lessie and laid them on her chest, right where her internal heat core was. My clothes began to steam almost immediately, and a few minutes later, they were completely dry. I pulled them on, then strapped on my weapons while Lessie wolfed down her kill.

Serpol returned to the clearing without Muza, his eyes glittering. "Good, you are clean," he said. "Come with me."

I climbed onto Lessie's back, and the three of us took to the skies. I lifted my face to the sun, savoring the rush of the wind across my skin and Lessie's warm body shifting beneath me. Both were experiences I'd never expected to enjoy again, and I felt blessed to be alive.

"Look." Serpol directed my attention to the archipelago below. From this vantage point I could see ten of the islands, the largest three grouped in the middle. The ones that stretched out below formed into an 'S' shape, and I wondered if the others coiled the same way, like a serpent. "This has been our home for the past two thousand years. As you can see, there is no human civilization whatsoever, save for the treehouse we allowed Varrick to build when he came here with Muza. You are only the second human to visit this place."

Varrick? Oh, he meant Tavarian. I wasn't used to referring to him by first name, even though we were engaged. "It's an honor to be invited here," I said gravely.

"*You weren't invited here,*" Serpol corrected. "*Muza brought you here without consulting us. But you were dying, and he told us that you are Varrick's mate, so my mother saved you. Come, she is waiting for us.*"

We flew toward the biggest of the three main islands, a tropical paradise with clear blue lagoons and waterfalls cascading down the hillsides. As we drew closer, I could see there were dragons everywhere, lazing around on clifftops, playing in the water, racing through the fields and forests. We passed a trio of baby dragons who were practicing their flying skills by leaping off a large boulder and coasting to the ground, carefully supervised by their mother. A half mile away, two dragons curled up in the sun together, their tails entwined.

Families, I realized, a little dazed. The dragons here had families. Their eggs weren't taken away to hatch and bond to a human. They were born with, and raised by, their mothers. They got to grow up with their siblings—and to play and learn under the guidance of their parents. Just like humans.

Serpol landed in a clearing right next to a huge waterfall, where a giant green dragon waited. *"My mother, Yalora,"* he said as I slid off Lessie's back.

"Pleased to meet you." I looked up at her. Then, not sure what else to do, I bowed. "Thank you for saving my life."

Yalora chuckled. *"A human bowing to a dragon? I'll bet your fellow Elantians would be scandalized."* Her gold eyes glittered in amusement. *"I like you, dragon rider. I can see why Varrick chose you as his mate."*

I cleared my throat. "Are you the...umm...leader of the free dragons?"

Yalora snorted. *"We have no leader. After Zakyiar was banished from this world, we agreed to never again be bound by a single ruler. We have what you might call a council of sorts, that meets every so often to discuss important matters and handle disputes, but overall we leave each other to our own devices."*

"I see." I glanced up to see two adult dragons flying past with four adolescents on their tails. "Just how many dragons are here, anyway?"

"A little less than a thousand," Yalora said. *"Perhaps one day we may outgrow these islands and see the need to expand our territory, but for now this archipelago is more than enough. And it must remain shielded from outsiders."*

"I won't tell a soul about this place," I said. "You have my word."

"Good." Yalora seemed satisfied. *"Now, come here and let me examine you."*

Bemused, I walked over to Yalora. She touched her snout to my forehead, and power washed through me, a tingling sensation that made me shiver. Suddenly, I was aware of how fatigued and achy I was, and I sat down heavily on the ground, my legs no longer able to support my weight.

"As I suspected." Yalora pulled away. *"You are still recovering. A few good nights' rest should have you sorted, as long as you don't do anything strenuous."*

She checked Lessie in the same way, then shook her head. *"Lessie, on the other hand, needs at least two weeks to fully heal her damaged lungs. It was extremely foolish, what she did, diving into that miasma without any protection. But, under the circumstances, it was understandable. The two of you did us a great favor by destroying that piece of the dragon god's heart, so, as far as I am concerned, you are friends to our kind. You may stay here as long as you need."*

"Thank you," I said, doing my best not to show my dismay. Two weeks? We'd already been gone for nearly a month! I needed to know what was happening back at Polyba. I needed to know if my fellow dragon riders were safe, if Tavarian had secured the alliance, and if the Zallabarians had tried to attack us yet.

"Muza is trying his best to contact Tavarian," Lessie said, sensing my distress. She curled up around me, tucking me against her giant body. *"He will tell us as soon as he has an update."*

"Good." That was the best I could hope for. Yawning, I leaned against Lessie's warm, scaly hide and settled in. "I'm ready for a nap."

"Sleep, then." Yalora's voice echoed in my head. I looked up at her through hazy eyes just in time to see her snap out her wings, preparing for flight. *"You need your rest, and this is as good a place as any. No harm will come to you. You have my word."*

Nodding, I closed my eyes. The sound of beating wings and Lessie's deep breathing lulled me off to sleep, and I slipped into the darkness, saving my worries for another day.

TWO

Lessie and I spent most of that first day at the treehouse, sleeping off our exhaustion and waking only to eat or to relieve ourselves. The next few days passed in mostly the same way, with the dragons leaving us undisturbed. Much as I wanted to get back to Polyba, I was grateful for the gift of solitude. It gave me time to think, to rest, to give my weary mind and body a break after what seemed like months of non-stop worrying.

On the fourth day, Lessie and I made another trip out to the lake so I could bathe and wash my clothes. We were just about to leave when three dragons soared overhead, circled the pond, and then landed a few feet from us, kicking up dust with their wings.

I coughed and brushed at my clothes and hair, trying not to be irritated at the fresh film of dirt that covered me. "Hey," I said cautiously, eyeing the trio. Muza and Serpol I recognized, but there was a smaller dragon between them, this one with deep purple scales.

"*Good morning, Zara.*" Serpol inclined his head. "*This is Roocian, my sister and Muza's mate. She has been eager to meet you.*"

"Oh!" I blinked, startled, and took a closer look at the female dragon. With blue-tipped spikes and crystal-clear aquamarine eyes, Roocian was one of the most beautiful dragons I'd ever seen. Her purple scales shimmered like a sea of amethyst, and I was struck by a sudden urge to run my hand across them. "I didn't realize Muza had a mate. That's wonderful!"

"*The most beautiful dragon you've ever seen?*" Lessie asked, sounding mortally offended.

"*One of the most beautiful dragons I've ever seen,*" I hastily corrected, running a hand down Lessie's shimmering scales. "*She still doesn't hold a candle to you.*"

"*Wonderful?*" Roocian's voice rang out in my head, clear and bell-like. The scathing disdain in her tone shocked me, and I took a step back as she bared her teeth at me. "*Would you think it wonderful, if you were mated to someone who you knew could die at any time simply because he is enslaved to a weak human?*"

Muza growled at that, but Roocian ignored him. "You mean the dragon rider bond?" I asked, astounded. "Of course I know what that's like. All dragon riders live with that possibility."

Roocian tossed her head. "*Yes, but you dragon riders normally only live for a few hundred years at the most. Dragons, on the other hand, can live thousands of years. And yet the ones bound to you selfish humans have to give up those years, simply because of that stupid bonding spell.*"

"*Roocian,*" Serpol said in a warning tone. "*It is not the fault of the present-day dragon riders. They are not the ones who created the spell. And if they didn't bond to their dragons then those eggs never would have hatched.*"

"*If it bothers you so much, why did you mate yourself to Muza?*" Lessie snapped, her temper fraying. "*You knew what he was when you chose this, didn't you?*"

"*I did, but that was before Elantia embroiled itself in another war and Varrick started putting his life at risk again!*" Roocian snarled, snapping her teeth at Lessie. She leveled a glare at me that was so potent I was surprised I wasn't incinerated on the spot. "*Now the centuries I should have with Muza may be reduced to days. How am I supposed to lay eggs under these circumstances, when there is a genuine possibility that the hatchlings may never see their father?*"

Lessie snorted. "*I never saw my father, or my mother, and I turned out fine.*"

Roocian drew herself upright. "*You are not a free dragon. You will never know what it is like to be one of us.*"

Muza growled again, the sound more threatening this time, and Roocian ducked her head, looking abashed. Obviously he didn't appreciate that statement, since Muza himself wasn't technically a free dragon either.

"You're right, Roocian," I said, taking a step toward her. She turned her head to face me, and I swallowed as she pinned me with that resentful gaze. "You have every right to be upset about Muza's bond with Tavarian. We've all come close to death quite a few times these past months. But I'm not really sure what I can do to fix that. Tavarian isn't going to go into hiding just to protect his and Muza's lives. We have to defeat the Zallabrians and take the country back so they don't enslave our dragons and use them for their own nefarious purposes."

"Enslave your dragons?" Roocian sounded skeptical. *"They are already enslaved. How can they be enslaved twice?"*

"The Zallabarians have been stealing dragon eggs and kidnapping dragon-rider children," I explained. "They plan on raising their own dragon-rider force, it would seem." Why the autocrator wanted to do this, I had no clue. The Zallabarians on the whole hated dragons with a passion, and I knew from my time there that most of them would rather kill all the dragons than raise them for their own purposes.

"So you are merely saying that they will trade one master for another." Roocian rolled her eyes. *"It would be far better to simply free the dragons from their bond. That way the Zallabarians would not be able to use them, and they wouldn't have to die prematurely."*

"Free them?" I echoed. "How?"

"By breaking the tie, of course," Roocian said matter-of-factly. *"My mother and Serpol have been working on a spell to do just that. We were hoping to test it on you and Lessie."*

"What?" Lessie and I instinctively recoiled. Dissolving our dragon bond? But how would we be able to communicate, to read each other's thoughts and feelings, to know when the other was in trouble? We'd only been bonded for a year, but the concept of breaking the connection between us was unthinkable.

A giant shadow fell over us, and Yalora landed in the clearing, making the ample space quite crowded with so many dragons. *"What is going on here?"* she demanded. *"Zara and Lessie are supposed to be resting."*

"I am talking to them about the spell," Roocian explained. "They are going to volunteer."

"Now wait a minute!" I snapped, annoyed at Roocian's heavy-handed demeanor. "I didn't agree to any of that! I'm still trying to wrap my head around the concept."

"Even if she did agree, Zara and Lessie are in no condition to undergo an experimental magical procedure," Yalora said in that severe tone mothers used on naughty children. *"The two of them are still recovering from a near-death experience!"*

Roocian bristled, and I imagined that between her and Serpol, she'd been the rebellious child. *"I am not saying they need to do it now, Mother,"* she said, sounding exasperated. *"But surely once they are ready...?"*

"The spell still needs work, and it is not the priority," Yalora said. *"We must first work on perfecting the shield."*

"Shield?" I asked. "What shield?"

"When Muza told us there was a possibility the dragon god would return, Serpol and I began work on a shielding spell that would protect us from his influence. I was alive during the Dragon War, and I remember what it was like to be under Zakyiar's control. He was a terrible taskmaster and allowed us no autonomy or free will. If he came back, he would use his powers to enslave us again. The shield will prevent that from happening."

"Well, that's good, but now that I've destroyed part of the

dragon god's heart, there's no way he'll be able to come back," I pointed out. "How exactly would this bond-severing spell work?"

Yalora stared at me for a long minute before answering. *"Serpol and I have studied the bond between Muza and Tavarian extensively. The original mage who cast the spell was foolish and self-centered and did not consider the ramifications of bonding dragons and mages so closely. Unfortunately, the magic is very powerful, and there is no way to undo it completely. However, we could alter it and replace it with what I like to think of as a friendship bond."*

"Friendship bond?" Lessie perked up. *"That sounds much better than breaking the bond completely. What would it entail?"*

"It would be more like a mutual support pact," Serpol explained. *"It is actually quite similar to the mating bond between dragons. The two of you would still be able to share thoughts and feelings through the mental link, but you would no longer be soul-bound, and Lessie would be able to converse freely with other humans, like we can. This would also mean freeing Lessie from the compulsion to act on your will. You would no longer be able to force her to obey your commands."*

Lessie and I exchanged looks. *"Zara has rarely exerted that sort of influence on me anyway,"* she said, *"so it doesn't seem like we're losing anything if we go through with this."*

Muza huffed loudly, nudging his mate, and Roocian turned to him, engaging in silent conversation.

"Muza doubts the spell would work and says it isn't worth the risk in his eyes," Lessie relayed to me. *"He feels that Tavari-*

an is a great partner and doesn't mind being bonded to him," she added, and Roocian bared her teeth. *"Since the spell requires the consent and presence of both parties, Muza would have to talk to Tavarian about it, and he doesn't want to bring it up. He thinks it would be insulting to their partnership."*

I frowned. "I don't think Tavarian would be insulted at all." More likely, Muza felt guilty about severing the bond. But wouldn't it be easier on both of them if he did, since they couldn't be together? Whenever I was away from Lessie, I ached fiercely for her presence. I couldn't imagine what it must be like for Muza and Tavarian being separated all these years. Perhaps changing the bond would make it more bearable.

"Zara and I would like to volunteer for the experiment," Lessie announced.

"We...we would?" I gaped at her. "Lessie, are you sure?" Sure, it sounded good in theory, but this was all so sudden! What if something went wrong? What if we regretted it?

"Zara," Lessie said, nuzzling my side. *"I nearly died at the Hellmouth and would have taken you with me if not for Serpol and Yalora. What is the point of rescuing you or coming to your aid if putting myself in danger only means we will both die? Wouldn't it be better if we were both freed from that burden? Look how many times Salcombe was able to control you because you didn't want me to die along with you. This soul bond is a terrible weakness. It will be much better for both of us if we can eradicate it."*

I wanted to argue, but I remembered how I'd nearly been gored by that boar a few days ago. If Lessie hadn't come to the rescue, we would have both died. And that hadn't even been in battle. By our very nature, the two of us lived dangerous, unpredictable lives.

"Besides," Lessie added, a little slyly, *"if we can prove the spell works, then Muza won't have any reason to pussyfoot around the subject. He and Tavarian can do the procedure, and then he and Roocian can raise a whole brood of dragonlings together."*

"Exactly." Roocian sounded pleased. *"I am glad to see someone around here is sensible."*

"You two would make stunning babies," I said, admiring them. They made a handsome pair, Muza with his silver scales and black-tipped spikes, and Roocian with her amethyst and robin's egg blue. I wondered if the dragonlings they made would each take after one parent or if there would be a mix of their characteristics. Purple and silver? Blue and black? Something else? I wished I knew more about how dragon genes were passed on.

Muza chuffed an amused sound, and I caught the wistful look in his eye.

"You really do want to be a father, don't you?" I asked, feeling sympathetic for him. How long had he and Roocian been together? He must have felt so conflicted when they'd been mated, knowing that he wouldn't be able to be there for the rest of her life. If Lessie and I could help him change that, this would all be worth it.

Plus, now that I knew free dragons could speak freely, I realized how annoying it was that Muza and Lessie couldn't. How much easier would our lives be if humans and dragons could converse without having to filter the messages through their partners? It would be especially handy in the war, where time was of the essence.

"*Not to mention it would remind the other humans that dragons are intelligent beings,*" Lessie said. "*Too many of them think we are stupid, mindless creatures, mere commodities that can be used to do their bidding.*"

"Right." I turned back to Yalora. "I'm in agreement with Lessie. We should do it."

As the dragons discussed the logistics amongst themselves, I leaned against Lessie and pressed my cheek against her warm hide. In the back of my mind, a warning itched that this might very well shorten my life span. But if this spell ensured that Lessie got to live a long, happy life, then Yalora could take as many of my years as she needed.

Over the next week, Lessie and I focused on recovering, exploring the island, and learning as much as we could from the dragons. Well, Lessie was the one who did the learning. When she wasn't sleeping, she spent much of her time with Serpol, practicing techniques to shield her mind from the influence of the dragon god. Despite my assurances that Zakyiar wasn't coming back, the other dragons weren't convinced. The older ones who had lived through the Dragon War were especially paranoid.

"Zakyiar may not be able to resurrect his body now that you've destroyed one of the pieces of his heart and entrusted the other to the death god," Yalora said to me at one point over dinner, "but his disciple still has three pieces, and that is more than enough to do significant damage. We must be prepared for any eventuality."

His disciple? I thought as I trekked through a jungle on one of the islands, following my treasure sense. It told me that there was a bevy of pearls here, hidden inside oyster shells, which meant there was a cove nearby. Yalora must have been referring to Salcombe. Part of me had hoped he'd died in our last confrontation, but the rest of me knew better. Even a hurricane on the high seas wasn't enough to stop Salcombe, not when he had three of the pieces of heart with him. The dragon god had probably protected him...

"But what if he didn't?" Lessie pointed out. *"Or, maybe he did, but what if Zakyiar is angry at Salcombe for his failure? After all, he will never be able to reunite all the pieces now. It's possible he's deserted Salcombe and left the old man to waste away. Without the dragon god's powers, his health will fade, especially at the rate he's been pushing his body."*

"True." The thought of Salcombe holed up somewhere, forced to suffer as his body decayed, filled me with great satisfaction. But I knew better than to trust in that fantasy too much. I'd believe Salcombe was dead when I saw it with my own two eyes.

The sound of waves crashing against the shore distracted me from my thoughts, and I quickened my pace. The air changed, becoming brinier, and my treasure sense chimed louder. Trees parted to reveal a small cove sheltered by a protective circle of rocky outcroppings. The sand was pure white, the water was a teal almost too beautiful to be real. Entranced, I tugged off my clothing. The sand felt good against my bare feet, soft and powdery, and for a minute I was tempted to flop down and fall asleep there in nothing but my underwear.

But the pearls tugged at my treasure sense, beckoning me closer. And I'd never been one to resist the lure of treasure.

I set my clothes on a sunny rock, then used a strip of cloth I'd torn from my shirt to fasten one of my daggers to the outside of my leg. I wasn't making the mistake of going into the water unarmed, not after that incident with the boar.

I waded into the ocean, savoring the feel of the warm water lapping against my bare skin. Maybe later I'd do some laps, float on my back and stare up at the sun while it baked my already tanned flesh. My body thrumming with eagerness, I sucked in a deep breath of salty air and dove beneath the waves.

The sounds of the open air disappeared, replaced by the pressure of the water rushing past my ears as I swam. The salt stung my eyes, so I tried keeping them closed at intervals, but it was so damn beautiful down here. Colorful fish darted between fronds of seaweed and shells of all shapes and sizes sparkled on the floor. The oysters weren't far, only a few more feet down.

I reached the bottom and started digging, my treasure sense pinging loudly now. *Jackpot*, I cheered silently as I pulled an oyster out of the sand. It was giant, dwarfing my hand. Tucking it under my arm, I dug around for a few more. My hand closed around a hard and bumpy rock, and I tugged on it.

A huge creature reared out of the sand, the eyes I had taken for pebbles flying wide open. I screamed, losing half my air in the process, and let go of its snout. It was enormous, twelve feet long and covered in fish scales, but with a reptilian body and short, stubby legs. The thing lunged for me, and I dodged, barely escaping its sharp teeth.

"Zara!" Lessie's alarmed voice rang out in my head. *"What's happening?"*

I didn't answer her—I was too busy fighting for my life. I

kicked for the surface, pumping my arms and legs as fast as I could. Teeth closed around my calf, sending a sharp pain through the limb, and I yanked my knife from my improvised thigh sheath and lashed out angrily. The creature reared back, its snout slashed open. Clouds of blood spewed from both of our wounds, muddling the waters and giving everything a reddish haze. My lungs were desperate for air and I felt dizzy.

Ignoring the pain, I struggled upward again, hoping against hope that the creature wouldn't follow. Just as I neared the surface, a clawed hand reached into the water and scooped me up out of the ocean.

"Lessie!" I gasped, gratefully gulping in the fresh air. The wind rushed past me as we flew away from the beach, chilling my wet skin.

"*What were you doing down there by yourself?*" she snapped. "*You could have gotten killed!*"

"*I was searching for treasure!*" Forlornly, I looked back at the cove. I'd dropped the oyster while fleeing, and I sure as hell wasn't going back for it. "*My treasure sense told me there were pearls down there.*"

Lessie huffed. "*And what good will they do you here? I know you must be bored, Zara, especially since there aren't any books on the island, but at least bring Muza with you next time if I'm not around.*"

I sighed. I wasn't used to the idea of having a babysitter, but Lessie was right, and I couldn't afford to risk my life so carelessly. All the more reason for us to sever the soul bond, right?

Serpol used his magic to heal my leg wound, and, for the rest of the week, I stayed out of trouble. Yalora took pity on me and brought me to the nursery island—a smaller island toward the outskirts of the archipelago that the dragons vigorously guarded—and allowed me to play with the baby dragons. Unlike Lessie at their age, most of them were too young to have fully developed language, and their mental skills weren't strong enough to hold conversations with me. Of course, they had spent a much shorter time inside their eggs. Still, it was great fun to run around in the fields with them, playing tag and tickling their warm, scaly bellies.

Finally, on my eighth day since waking up in the treehouse, Yalora and Serpol declared that the spell was ready to be performed. Lessie and I joined them along with Muza and Roocian on the beach at sunset. The other dragons stood in a half-circle, their gazes solemn as they waited for us to land.

"Thank you for doing this," Roocian said to me, inclining her head. *"It means a lot to my mate and me."*

Muza huffed out a breath through his nostrils.

"He says he still isn't sure he wants to do this ritual himself, even if it does work," Lessie translated, *"but if it can help other dragons and riders, he thinks it is worth trying."*

"I think you will want to do it," I told Muza gently, placing a hand on his snout. But he only sighed, nudging my hand, and I stood at the spot in the sand that Yalora indicated, Lessie at my side.

"Are you ready?" Serpol asked.

The two of us nodded. "We are," I said.

"Good. Then we shall begin."

The two dragon mages sprinkled strange herbs and rocks around us, enclosing us in a fragrant circle. *"Close your eyes,"* Yalora said, her voice soothing, almost hypnotic. I allowed my eyelids to drift shut, breathing in the scents of the sea and the herbs, taking in the sounds of the dragons breathing, the waves crashing against the surf, gulls crying out as they flew over the sea, searching for their next meal.

Yalora and Serpol began to chant in a melodic language, strange words flowing through my head that didn't sound like any language I'd ever heard. I tried not to worry about their meaning, and instead let the sounds ebb and flow through my mind, taking me farther and farther away...

Suddenly, I wasn't standing on the beach anymore. I was on a hillside, standing next to a strange man. He was solidly built, with salt and pepper hair and striking violet eyes that scanned the skies as he crouched in the tall grass. As I studied him, I noticed that he wore dark purple mage robes, and clutched a thick tome in his hand. His other hand was buried in the dirt, and when I inched closer to get a better look, I saw that it was glowing, the light muffled by the earth and grass around him. Power crackled through the air, and I shivered, the hairs on my arms rising in warning.

"Hello?" I crouched down next to him. "Can you hear me?"

The man didn't respond, not even when I waved a hand in front of his face. Frowning, I debated kicking dirt at him to see what would happen when a roar split the sky. My heart drummed in my chest as I looked skyward to see a golden dragon emerge from the clouds, its snout pointed toward the lake nestled at the bottom of the hillside.

"That's it," the man shouted, his violet eyes sparkling with anticipation. "Come on, you great big beast!" He jumped up, waving his arms, and my heart leaped into my throat as the dragon altered course. I jumped out of the way, not wanting to become barbecue, but a huge purple disc flared into existence right above the man's head. The dragon's snout struck the disc, and the magical energy began to unravel into what looked like a giant, glowing net.

"Gotcha!" the mage crowed, and I stared open-mouthed as the dragon thrashed, trying to escape the net. But the magical ropes snapped into place before she could find an opening, and the dragon crashed into the hillside and rolled all the way to the base of the lake.

Dragon's balls. My knees gave out, and I collapsed into the dirt as the mage sprinted down the hillside. Sweat beaded on his forehead as he opened up the tome he was holding, and his entire body trembled as he closed his hand around one of the magical ropes. This was probably the closest he'd ever been to a dragon in his life, and judging by the murderous look in the captive dragon's eyes, he had every right to be afraid.

Holding tight to the rope, the mage used his other hand to flip through the book's pages until he came to one that had been dog eared and marked up so many times the original writing was barely visible. "Come on, Akron," he panted, his eyes wild with fear and excitement. "You can do this."

Akron the Defender. The mage who had bound a dragon to himself, and created the dragon rider race. My mind went numb as I struggled to process this. I'd thought I was dreaming, but this dream was more real than anything I'd ever conjured in my mind before. Had I traveled back in time? Was I witnessing a piece of history?

The dragon roared, and I expected Akron to scamper away with his tail between his legs, like any sensible person would have done. But the display of rage only seemed to strengthen his resolve, and he straightened his spine and began chanting in an ancient tongue. With each word he spoke, the rope in his hand seemed to grow longer, and he sucked in a sharp breath as it slowly inched up his arm, twisting round and round the limb, past his shoulder and beyond. The dragon struggled mightily against the binding, but Akron held firm, his voice growing louder and louder as the glowing ropes twisted around his entire body. At the same time, the net continued to tighten around the dragon, until I could no longer see either of them.

Akron the Defender shouted one last word, and a thunder-clap rent the sky. Light exploded from them both, knocking me back—

I GASPED, my eyes flying wide open to take in the beach once more. It was full dark now, the sunset long gone, replaced by inky skies and twinkling stars. Yalora and Serpol sat directly in front of us, their shoulders slumped, while Muza and Roo-cian stood off to the side.

Lessie jerked next to me, as if she'd woken from a dream as well. *"What happened?"* she cried. *"Has the soul bond been undone?"*

"I'm afraid not," Yalora said sadly. *"Serpol and I tried to undo it, but the connection between you two is too strong. Severing it would have killed you both."*

"Damn." I leaned my forehead against Lessie's shoulder, my

heart still racing. Part of me was relieved that nothing had changed—the bond between us was as strong as ever, and I could feel the emotions rushing through Lessie: elation, relief, guilt, disappointment. The same emotions I was feeling. But I was also sad that the ritual had failed. I had warmed up to the idea of not being soul-bound anymore—had almost been looking forward to it, in fact.

"*Oh well.*" Lessie shrugged, her tone very matter-of-fact. "*It was still worth trying anyway. And now that this is over with, you and I can get back to Polyba. It is past time we were reunited with our friends.*"

"Will you come with us?" I asked Muza. We needed all the help we could get, and I knew how happy Tavarian would be to have Muza by his side again.

Muza nodded his great head. "*We discussed it last night,*" Roocian told me. "*I am not happy about him leaving, but it is clear that this war needs to end before it is brought to our shores. From what I hear about the Zallabarians, they are like a disease, spreading to all corners of our world—it is only a matter of time before they infect us as well, and I would see that stopped.*"

"*As would I,*" Serpol said. "*Which is why I will come with you, too.*"

"You will?" I gaped up at him. "I mean, that's great and all—we could really use another dragon, and especially one who's a mage." Though I had no idea how we'd explain that to the others—or would we? Could we even keep Serpol's status as a 'free dragon' a secret? People would be wondering who his rider was. With such a small community, it was only a matter of time before the others figured out he didn't have one.

"Of course. Like Roocian said, we need to end this war. Besides, I want to study the situation of the captive dragons and riders more closely. Perhaps I will be able to pinpoint the issue with our spell."

Lessie bristled. Naturally, she hated the idea of being referred to as captive. But I put a hand on her shoulder, willing her to keep silent. Regardless of Serpol's reasoning for coming, he was a good asset to have. And if he could figure out how to make the spell work, so much the better for us.

FOUR

The next night, Lessie and I left with Muza and Serpol. I felt a pang of regret as I watched the archipelago shrink into the distance behind us—this past week had been peaceful, almost carefree, and I had enjoyed getting to know the free dragons better. I wondered if we would ever come back here...if Lessie and I survived the war, that was.

"It will not take us nearly as long to get to Polyba as it took you to come all the way out here," Serpol told us as we flew. *"Muza knows the best route to Elantia and says we should be able to make it back to the island within a week."*

"That's a relief." I was anxious to get back to my friends—Tavarian, Rhia, Halldor, Jallis. Rhia and Halldor would have told the others I was dead, and I couldn't bear the thought of them grieving needlessly. Not to mention there was still so much to be done.

We flew over the ocean, heading for the mainland, which Muza said was the faster route, contrary to what I had thought.

Apparently, he had regular camping spots and knew all the best hunting grounds, too. As I glanced down at the waves, which were tinged silver by the moonlight, I noticed three ships in the distance, their prows pointed straight toward the dragons' archipelago.

"*Aren't those warships?*" Lessie asked, a suspicious note entering her voice.

I pulled my goggles over my eyes and zoomed in on the ships. "They're not flying their nation's flag," I said, an uneasy pit forming in my stomach. "Could mean they're pirates, except there's nothing out here except for the archipelago."

"*Let's take a closer look,*" Serpol suggested. "*Find out what they're up to.*"

"How? It's not like we'll be able to hear anything unless we get close enough for them to spot us."

Serpol gave me a toothy grin. "*Watch and learn.*"

A silvery glow enveloped Serpol's body, and he beat his wings a few extra times. Silver dust swirled all around us, and I shivered as the power caressed my skin, covering me in a fine film. I thought it would settle there, but the magic disappeared quickly, absorbed by my body.

I gasped as my skin turned translucent, revealing the open ocean beneath me. No, not just my skin. Lessie's too! All four of us had become transparent. If I looked closely, I could see the outlines of the dragons who flew beside us, but only because they were right next to me. If Muza or Serpol flew away, I would never be able to follow them.

"*Neat trick, isn't it?*" Serpol winked at me. "*Now we can get as close as we like.*"

"No kidding." This was ten times better than Tavarian's camouflage spell, which only worked at certain distances.

The four of us dipped lower, each dragon flying around a different ship. The crash of the waves and the wind whistling in my ears still meant that I couldn't hear anything the sailors on the deck were saying, but the dragons had superior hearing and were able to eavesdrop easily.

"*Bastards,*" Lessie hissed as she relayed the information to me. "*These ships are from the Zallabarian fleet! They are here to claim the 'uninhabited' islands out here as Zallabarian colonies.*"

"*They plan to use our forests for timber to build more ships,*" Serpol added. "*And they mentioned something about big new expansion plans for their navy.*" He paused. "*What is a navy?*"

"*It's a section of a country's armed forces, specially trained to fight battles at sea.*" I gritted my teeth. So they wanted to come to the archipelago and steal its natural resources, did they? Not if I could help it.

"*Ahh. So that is why they need to build more ships.*" Serpol bared his teeth at the sails. "*Well, I for one will not stand by and let them attack the island. We need to head them off.*"

"Agreed," I said. "Let's torch these assholes."

The dragons were more than happy to do just that, and unleashed gouts of flame on the sails, masts, and decks. The sailors screamed in terror and confusion—all they saw were waves of fire, conjured out of thin air and rushing toward the ships. They probably thought they were being attacked by a rogue mage.

Which, in a way, was true.

As the scents of burning flesh and wood soured the evening

air, I tried not to think about the fact that there were men on board, burning alive. While I wouldn't wish such a death on anyone, this was war, and we couldn't let these men reach the archipelago. The Zallabarians wouldn't be able to tame the free dragons, which meant they would kill them. And though I had no doubt Yalora and her brethren could hold their own against the Zallabarians, word would spread. Other nations might team up in an effort to exterminate the dragons. After all, people hated and feared what they didn't understand, and the world saw dragons as instruments of war and oppression. Not as a sentient species, intelligent, compassionate, and just as deserving of life as the rest of us.

Once the ships were reduced to flaming piles of wood, slowly sinking into the ocean, the four of us took to the skies again. Hidden by the clouds once more, Serpol released the spell.

"Why not just keep it on us?" I asked.

"It taxes my energy," Serpol explained, "and since I am flying, I need as much strength as I can get."

"Right." Tavarian had held his invisibility spell for hours, but he'd merely been riding, not actually flying himself. Of course it would be harder on Serpol, who was expending constant physical effort. The fact that dragons could fly for hours on end, that they had such tremendous stamina, was amazing. Something I often took for granted.

"Well, we are the superior species," Lessie said smugly, and I laughed.

As we traveled, Lessie and I did our best to explain the war between Elantia and Zallabar, and the background of both nations to Serpol.

"*What nonsense,*" he said when we'd finished telling him about Zallabar's plans. "*I will never understand this human desire to steal territory. It is one thing to guard your own territory fiercely, but so long as your people have enough, why is there any reason to kill and steal from others?*"

I sighed. "There are many reasons, but as far as I'm concerned, none of them are good."

Serpol nodded. "*In any case, I agree that you cannot allow Zallabar to take your country, and that the...bound...dragons—*" he chose his words carefully this time, mindful of Lessie—"*are at risk so long as they are in your lands. Since this autocrator was foolish enough to send his ships to our archipelago, it would seem we have a common enemy.*"

Over the next ten days, Muza led us overland, past many countries and terrains I'd never seen before. We camped near bogs full of purple mist, in deserts slithering with snakes and other reptilian creatures, and in forests of towering trees with trunks as wide as airships. No matter where we stopped for the night, there was always game to hunt or fish to catch, as Muza had promised. And thanks to Serpol and his protective magic, I never had to worry about the elements or predators while we slept.

"*Finally,*" Lessie crowed as the island came into view. I never thought the sight of Polyba would fill me with such joy and relief. The place was made up of harsh terrain, mostly brush and rocks and thorns, with very little water or game to hunt—not to mention it was populated by hostile locals who, until recently, were trying to kill us. But we'd made peace with some of the locals and figured out how to make the land work for us. And now that we had an airship and dragons, it was all too easy to ferry supplies back and forth, turning the once forsaken island into an effective base of operations.

An effective base that, I now noticed, was under attack.

"Warships coming from the southwest!" I shouted, pointing at the fleet heading straight for the narrow beach closest to our base. Zooming in with my goggles, I saw that the decks were absolutely packed with soldiers armed with muskets and swords. The ships themselves also bristled with cannons, and while the estate we were using as our base was too far from the shore to be hit directly, they would kill many of the Elantian soldiers gathered on the beach, waiting for the enemy to strike. Dragons circled the island, roaring in frustration—they didn't dare get close for fear of being struck down by the Zallabarians' deadly shrapnel cannons, specifically crafted to shred dragon wings.

"Where are you going?" I cried as Muza winged off to the east, speeding away from the island. One of the ships turned their cannons toward him, but he dodged the projectile without slowing.

"He is going to Tavarian," Serpol told me. *"Don't worry about him. Let us do something about these ships!"*

Serpol flapped his wings again, generating more magic dust. But instead of coating us, the dust swirled around, then solidified into a glowing barrier. Lessie reared back as a cannonball barreled toward us, only for the projectile to explode harmlessly against the shield.

"They cannot harm us," Serpol said, tucking his wings in at his sides. *"Let's go!"*

Lessie followed suit, and I held on for dear life as the two dragons dove toward the ships. There were at least forty vessels of varying sizes, a formidable armada. As we bombarded them with fireballs and shredded their sails, a few of the other dragons tried to join in, but Lessie and Serpol ordered them back. We couldn't afford to lose these dragons, not after all the trouble we'd gone through to rescue them from the Zallabarians' clutches.

We managed to disable ten of the ships before Serpol's shield began to flicker. *"We need to retreat,"* he panted as a cannonball broke through. Lessie dodged left, and my breath froze in my lungs as the projectile whizzed right by my head. *"My magic is nearly depleted—the shield won't hold for much longer."*

"Dammit!" I surveyed the fleet with dismay as we climbed higher into the sky, out of range of the remaining ships. The ten we'd destroyed were useless now: their sails wrecked, the decks on fire, their cannons melted into slag. But there were still thirty more ships left, and though they'd temporarily pulled back, it was only a matter of time before they took advantage of our retreat. Was there anything we could do to stop them?

"Zara, look!" Lessie swung her head east, in the direction Muza had flown off to.

I looked in the same direction, and my stomach dropped at the sight of Muza flying toward us, with two dozen or so warships at his back. More enemies? I zoomed in with my goggles, and my heart jumped in my chest as I saw Tavarian aboard Muza's back, his black hair whipping in the wind as they flew. I hadn't seen him at first because his silver-scaled dragon-rider leathers made him blend in perfectly with Muza's hide.

Lessie stiffened beneath me, and she and Serpol turned tail, racing away from the island.

"*What are you doing?*" I cried, clutching one of Lessie's spikes. Shouldn't we be helping them?

"*Muza said that Tavarian is about to attack the fleet,*" Lessie said as the wind screamed in my ears. "*He told us to get out of the way as fast as we could!*"

Glancing back, I saw that Tavarian and Muza were closing in fast, much faster than the ships behind them. Tavarian pulled something out of his bag, and my entire body went rigid as I recognized the magical horn we'd found on Polyba. The secret weapon a dragon rider had hidden here long ago, one capable of reducing mountains to rubble.

"Crap!" I clapped my hands over my ears as Tavarian blew the horn.

The sound that issued forth was horrific, a terrible blare that shook the air. Lessie and I had been rendered senseless by it the first time Tavarian had used it, and I half expected Muza to drop out of the sky. But the silver dragon remained steady, flapping his wings to maintain his position as Tavarian continued to blow the horn.

The effect was almost instantaneous. The ships at the front of the armada exploded, blood and flesh, splinters and shrapnel, flying into the ocean at deadly speeds. Tavarian blew the horn again and again, obliterating more ships, turning the sea a frothy, angry red as the pulverized soldiers bled out into the ocean to become fodder for sharks and sea monsters. I shuddered, a large part of me disgusted and horrified at the carnage.

And yet, I was glad to see that the bastards had gotten what they deserved.

Several beats of heavy silence followed as we all watched the remnants of the ships sink into the water. But then whoops went up from the soldiers on the shore, and the dragons who had been circling trumpeted, shooting streams of celebratory flame into the sky.

"That was...unexpected," Serpol said, a little dazed as he stared down at the wreckage. *"I've never seen such terrible magic before."*

Tavarian finally lowered the horn, looking both harried and satisfied at once. My heart swelled at the sight of him, and Lessie sped toward Muza, sensing my intentions. I leaped off her back as she passed over the bigger dragon, and Tavarian, alarmed, caught me in his lap.

"Zara!" His silvery eyes widened, his hard-planed face slack with shock. "You could have killed yourself! Do you have any idea how deadly Muza's spikes are?"

"I knew you'd catch me." Throwing my arms around his neck, I kissed him hard, pouring weeks of frustration and longing into the kiss. Tavarian crushed me against his chest, kissing me back, and my heart sang with joy as the taste and scent of him filled me, surrounded me, sweeping away my doubts and fears and replacing them with stormy passion. There was a part of me that wanted to drag him off to some hideaway, a cozy inlet or a dark cave, and make love to him until both our minds and bodies gave out through sheer exhaustion.

Instead, I pulled away, breathing hard.

Tavarian gripped my face in his long-fingered hands. "I love you," he said, pressing his forehead against mine. His cheeks were flushed, his hair windswept, his eyes wild and blazing—completely different from the cool façade he presented to the world. This was a side of him that only *I* got to see, and I relished the moments when he dropped the mask and allowed me these precious glimpses of the real him.

"And I love you." I rubbed noses with him, soaking in the warmth of his body. We might have sat there like that forever if Muza hadn't craned his neck around to stare at us out of baleful eyes, huffing impatiently.

Tavarian chuckled. "Muza says that we should continue our reunion on the beach. He also says that he deserves a little more than a hello, too, since he flew all this way to see me."

I smiled. "Muza is right," I said, patting his hide. I called for Lessie, and she drew up alongside us so I could climb onto her back and let Muza and Tavarian land separately. The other dragon riders would be shocked to see that Tavarian had a dragon, since they'd long believed Muza was dead.

But Tavarian did not go back to the island. Instead, he returned to the ships that he and Muza had been leading here.

"*Warosian warships,*" Lessie explained as I used my goggles to zoom in on their flags. "*Muza says that Tavarian secured the alliance, and they loaned him these ships to help combat the invasion. Still, if not for us, he'd never have gotten here fast enough to use the horn in time.*"

Three dragons winged their way toward us. As they came closer, I saw it was Ykos, Kiethara, and Kadryn, with Rhia, Halldor, and Jallis astride their backs. "Zara!" the three of them cried at once, drawing up alongside Lessie to hover.

"Hey, guys!" I grinned at all three of them. "Surprised to see me?"

Rhia rolled her eyes, and I imagined she would have thrown something at me if there'd been a non-deadly object at hand. "We thought you were dead!" she shouted over the wind.

"Who's the new dragon?" Jallis asked, nodding at Serpol who was hovering nearby.

"Muza's friend Serpol," I shouted back. "The two of them arrived just in the nick of time to rescue us. They helped us get away from the island and back here."

"Muza is Tavarian's dragon?" Halldor asked. "I thought Tavarian didn't have a dragon anymore!"

"And who does Serpol belong to?" Rhia wanted to know.

Serpol snorted at that, and I hid a wince. "That's a long story we don't have time for." We'd already agreed that Serpol wouldn't speak directly to any human other than Tavarian and me—there was no way to explain that without admitting the existence of the free dragons. "We need to search the wreckage, just in case."

The four of us split up, joining the other dragon riders who were already circling the destroyed armada. As I'd suspected, there was nothing left but bits of floating wood and body parts. The ruined heads bobbing in the water were the worst, but there were only a few—I imagined most of them had exploded.

"At least they died quickly," Lessie pointed out. *"Which is more than they would have given us if they'd made it to shore."*

Leaving the others to pick through the remains, I returned

to Tavarian, who was on deck on one of the Warosian warships floating just offshore, speaking to the captain while Muza waited on the beach. Lessie dropped me next to Tavarian, and went to wait with Muza while Tavarian brought me up to speed.

"Zara." Tavarian inclined his head to me. "This is Admiral Petro Messei, the King of Warosia's cousin. Admiral, this is Commandant Zara Kenrook, leader of the Elantian Patriots."

I blinked—I hadn't realized we'd chosen a name for ourselves—but quickly masked my surprise. "It's a pleasure to meet you, Admiral." I stuck out my hand.

The admiral shook it, his blue eyes twinkling. "I have heard much about the fiery redhead who stole a fleet of dragons right beneath Autocrator Reichstein's nose," he said, and I blushed. He was a handsome man with curling blond hair and tanned skin, and he cut a fine figure in his naval uniform. "The pleasure is all mine."

"Indeed." Tavarian's expression was bland as dry toast, but there was a subtle undercurrent of warning in his tone that made the admiral drop my hand and take a step back. "The Admiral is here as an ambassador, and also to provide naval support for our war efforts."

"Yes, though I half-wonder if you'll even need us, after that impressive display back there." The admiral tried for levity, but his gaze flicked to the carnage still floating in the water, and his swarthy complexion paled. "You understand I need assurances that you will never use that terrible weapon against us."

"Of course not," Tavarian said, his tone turning solicitous. "You were there when I signed the alliance treaty. So long as neither side breaks the terms, you and I have nothing to fear from each other."

Tavarian and I invited the admiral to join us for our next council meeting, then returned to the island on Muza's back.

"Commandant! Lord Tavarian!" Captain Ragorin grinned as he strode toward us. "You're both a sight for sore eyes. Arrived just in the nick of time!"

"We sure did. How is everything, Captain?" I asked as I jumped off Muza's back. Six-foot-tall with a trim black beard and keen blue eyes, he was the leader of the Elantian soldiers that had escaped a Zallabarian POW camp and joined us dragon riders on Polyba. While at first we'd groaned at the idea of taking on several hundred more mouths to feed, the soldiers proved more than worth their keep—they'd ruthlessly organized our base, turning the crumbling mansion we'd been hiding out in into a real, defensible fort. Not to mention the additional forces gave the locals a healthy respect for us.

"Fine, now that we've got a fleet to defend us, and that terrifying horn." He eyed Tavarian. "I gather you found someone to teach you how to use it in Warosia?"

Tavarian nodded. "There is a mage scholar in the capital who specializes in ancient, mythical weapons. She taught me the secret to using it."

"Is it something I can be taught as well?" Ragorin asked.

"I'm afraid not. Only mages can use it."

Ragorin shook his head. "I still can't believe you're a mage," he muttered. Tavarian had kept that secret under wraps for a long time—a mage dragon-rider was unheard of—but after he'd started using his magic to heal wounded soldiers, there was no hiding it anymore. Ragorin glanced at Muza, who was waiting nearby. "I guess you're going to tell me that your dragon hasn't actually been dead all this time?"

Tavarian laughed. "It's a lot to take in, isn't it?"

"That's an understatement if I've ever heard one." Ragorin turned to me, wary now. "Are you at least going to tell me that you and Lessie were successful?"

"We were." I smiled. "The dragon heart pieces have been destroyed, and with them, any chance of the dragon god completing his resurrection."

"Thank the skies." Ragorin scrubbed a hand across his jaw, looking relieved. "Now I can sleep at night again."

The dragon riders finished searching the wreckage, and, with nothing else left to do on the beach, we returned to camp. Tavarian was quickly swept away by the soldiers, who laughed and cheered as they carried him back to base on their shoulders, ignoring his half-hearted protests. The man clearly wasn't used to such public admiration, not when he worked so hard to keep others at a distance, but he'd just saved everyone's asses, so he was just going to have to deal with it.

"You know," Halldor grumbled under his breath as we walked a little ways behind the crowd, "you should be up there with him. If not for you, we'd all be dead."

I shook my head. "I didn't do this for the praise, and besides, no one really needs to know just how close we were to annihilation." Let the soldiers have their celebration. With more battles looming on the horizon, I knew there were dark times ahead. We needed to take advantage of all the happy moments we could get.

When we arrived back at the estate, I was pleasantly surprised to see everything was even more organized than before. Over a thousand people were staying at the base now, with more Elantian refugees arriving every day. That meant more mouths to feed, but many of them were skilled laborers—carpenters, blacksmiths, seamstresses, cooks, farmers, and more. Captain Ragorin had wasted no time putting them all to work, and with new supplies coming in via airship on a regular basis, we were fast turning this formerly barren island into a real civilization.

"This is very impressive, Captain," I said as we toured the estate. "How are the natives taking all this...change?"

"They've come around," Captain Ragorin said with a grin. "Now that they've realized we're not the enemy, the clans have set up trade agreements. We practically have an unending supply of goat's milk and cheese now."

"That's great." But I knew that the natives didn't have

enough goats to keep us all fed, not with more and more Elantians arriving daily. We were going to have to start importing livestock, and grain to plant. But would there be enough water? Though the island was big, it certainly wasn't large enough to sustain the entire country of Elantia. We'd have to cut off new arrivals at some point, which I wasn't looking forward to at all.

"*We could expand to other islands,*" Lessie suggested. "*I know there are others not far from here that are uninhabited as well.*"

"*We could,*" I agreed, "*but we didn't come back here to colonize these outlying islands. We came back to win this war and take back our country. That's the real solution, and we can't lose sight of that.*"

Tavarian and I spent the rest of the day with the dragon riders and soldiers, getting caught up to speed. We also made sure the Warosian admiral and his crew had everything they needed. They'd decided to stay on their ships, but we gave them plenty of food and wine to supplement their rations. Though they'd proven unnecessary during this most recent battle, they made themselves useful now by patrolling the nearby waters for any more Zallabarian ships, and I knew we would need them in the future. Tavarian couldn't be everywhere at once with that horn, after all, and he was the only one who could use it.

By the time we stumbled back to our tower room, the two of us were well and truly exhausted. "I feel like I could sleep for a week," I groaned as I flopped onto the bed. "Can I sleep for a week?" I asked jokingly. "I think I deserve it."

Tavarian smiled as he removed his dragon rider armor, stripping down to the tight trousers and shirt he wore beneath. "You do deserve it," he agreed as he pulled off the shirt, too. My blood stirred at the sight of his bare torso, lean but well-muscled, with a light dusting of black hair that disappeared in a suggestive trail down the waistband of his trousers. His full mouth curled up at the corners as he noticed the look in my eyes, and he moved toward the bed. "But surely sleep isn't the only thing on your mind, is it?"

"Not anymore," I agreed as Tavarian pushed a curl away from my face. He kissed me, long and deep, then proceeded to slowly strip my armor off, kissing and nipping at each inch of skin he revealed. My exhaustion lifted, replaced by burning desire, and we made love fiercely, reveling in our shared passion, in the fact that we were both alive and well and together once again.

Well and truly spent, we fell asleep almost instantly, and for once, I didn't dream at all.

I wasn't sure how long I'd slept, but I woke at the sensation of fingers skimming along my side. Opening my eyes, I saw that I was lying on my side, facing Tavarian. The moonlight filtering in through the window limned his perfect face, which was soft with emotion. There was an almost dreamy quality to those silver eyes, and for a long moment we simply lay there, lost in each other's eyes.

Eventually, I reached out, tracing the keen edge of his cheekbone. "I saw you, when I visited the Underworld," I whispered. "It was just an illusion—part of a test—but it was so real that for a time I was afraid something had gone wrong, that the Warosians had killed you. I would have been devastated if Muza hadn't come to rescue us afterward."

Grief clouded Tavarian's eyes. "I *was* devastated when Halldor and Rhia sent word that you and Lessie hadn't made it out of the Hellmouth." He slid an arm around me, drew me close to his chest.

I leaned my head against his heart, letting the strong, steady beat soothe me.

"Muza sent me a message a few days later to let me know that he'd retrieved you and you were recovering on the island, which was the only thing that got me through these past weeks. When I saw him flying toward the Warosian fleet, it took everything I had not to jump on his back and fly straight to you instead of toward the enemy."

I briefly imagined kissing Tavarian on Muza's back, ignoring the world while the Zallabarians fired on our open shores, and cringe-laughed. "I'm glad you made the right choice on that one."

"Indeed." He rested his chin on the top of my head. "Tell me about the Hellmouth."

So I did. I told him about the pirates we'd hired to take us to the island, about the noxious gas, about the trials I'd had to face and the bargain I'd struck to get the death god to destroy one of the two pieces of Zakyiar's heart. The whole story came out in a rush, and by the time I finished I actually felt relieved. Finally, here was someone who I could share the entire experience with, someone who would not only believe me, but truly appreciate what I had gone through!

"Incredible." Tavarian shook his head, looking awed. "You actually met Derynnis himself. I do worry about what is going to become of the weapon he creates with the second piece of heart," he said. "Hopefully it doesn't find its way back to our world."

"I think he only gives them out very rarely, and since Derynnis hates the world of the living, I don't think we have to worry." Still, I shivered a little at the thought. A weapon powered by even a single piece of Zakyiar's heart would be mighty indeed.

I told Tavarian about our time with the free dragons, and the spell Yalora and Serpol had attempted to cast on Lessie and me. "It's too bad it didn't work, though," I said, a fresh wave of disappointment filling me. "If it had, Serpol could have done it on you and Muza, too."

"That would be quite something," Tavarian said. He looked dumbstruck at the possibility. "I'm amazed that Muza kept this from me. He and I are going to have to have a long talk about this tomorrow. There is nothing for him to feel guilty about—if there is a way for our souls to be safely separated, then of course we should take advantage of it so he can start a family and live a long, happy life. I will talk with Serpol tomorrow and see if we can collaborate on the spell. I picked up quite a few useful things during my time in Warosia—perhaps I can help figure out how to fix the problem."

"That would be great." I beamed, my heart swelling with hope. "How was Warosia, anyway? I gather the mage you met taught you more than just how to use the horn?"

"Oh yes. Arisa is very knowledgeable. She taught me how to activate the protective runes, and also how to angle the horn correctly. Apparently, it is best used from higher distances, which means the wielder must either be on dragonback or on an airship. If I'd used it from the admiral's ship, the blowback would have damaged his fleet."

"That would have been awful." My stomach twisted at the thought of the Warosians being caught in that blast. That would have ended our freshly minted alliance for sure. "What else did you learn?"

"A few spells here and there, but mostly more about magical theory and how to use my power more effectively. Arisa has an extensive library filled with magical texts, many of which I'd never seen before. I could have stayed for months, reading and learning." His eyes shone at the prospect.

A spurt of jealousy hit me, unexpectedly. "Months, huh?" I asked, sliding a hand along his biceps. "Just you and her and a pile of books?"

Tavarian frowned. "Preferably just the books," he said. "While quite helpful, Arisa is rather...bossy. I am not certain the two of us would make good housemates."

I raised my eyebrows. "You don't think I'm bossy?"

"You are, but in the right ways," he said teasingly.

"Good answer." I grinned, the jealousy dissipating as quickly as it had struck. "I'm glad you got what you needed from her. It scares me to think how bad things could have gone if you didn't arrive with that horn."

"Indeed. Though, I admit, it was horrifying to see it in action." A haunted look entered his eyes. "The magic ripped through those ships as if they were paper. It's been a long time since I've seen such carnage." He swallowed hard and looked away.

"It isn't your fault, Varrick." I cupped his cheek in my hand, making him meet my eyes. "It's the autocrator's, for sending them out there—for starting this whole stupid war in the first place. You did what needed to be done, and you saved hundreds of lives in the process."

Tavarian closed his eyes, leaning into my touch. "I agree. But I still regret having to kill so many men, especially now that I know many of them are unwilling conscripts."

"All the more reason to end this war as quickly as possible."

"Agreed."

We lay there in silence for a while, soaking in one another's presence. The sounds of our breath. The warmth of our bodies. The sensation of skin against skin. I'd nearly fallen asleep when Tavarian asked, "What do you think of getting married now?"

My eyes popped open. *"What?"*

Tavarian stared down at me, his expression solemn and intense all at once. "We nearly lost each other, Zara," he said, tightening his arms around me. "And every time we separate, I am acutely aware that we may not see each other again. I want to spend the rest of my life married to you, Zara. Even if that life might be cut short."

Tears pricked my eyes. "Don't talk like that," I said fiercely. "We're going to survive this war." But both of us had come close to death so many times that I had to admit Tavarian's fear wasn't unreasonable. "I want to marry you too, but the thought of having a ceremony and celebration in the middle of all this...and without Carina and the orphans...it doesn't seem right. At the very least I want them here with us."

Tavarian's brow furrowed. "Maybe we could have the ceremony at the Hidden Valley." We'd left the orphans there, at

Tavarian's secret estate, after a heartless investor had purchased the orphanage and kicked them all off the property.

I laughed. "You really do want to get married, don't you?"

He chuckled. "Yes, but I know how foolish that would be. And while the orphans might be tired of the hidden valley by now, Carina would never abandon your shop." Carina and I owned the Treasure Trove together, though lately it seemed more and more like it was her business and not mine since I hardly ever brought treasure back to the shop anymore. I felt guilty every time she paid me profits. Perhaps, when this was all over, I would let her buy me out for cheap. I'd still bring treasure to her—I was a treasure hunter at heart, after all—but I'd be like every other freelance hunter who brought wares to her. It didn't seem right to take so much of the profits when I wasn't putting in nearly the amount of work she was.

"*You can worry about the shop after we've taken the country back,*" Lessie said sleepily in my head. "*Now go to bed, Zara. Your thoughts are keeping me awake, and after all this travel I deserve some good rest.*"

"*Yes, you do.*" I smiled, snuggling in close with Tavarian, then closed my eyes and allowed myself to drift off. Tomorrow, the council would be meeting to hash out a plan of attack against the Zallabarians. Autocrator Reichstein had already proved to be a wily adversary; I would need all my wits about me if we were to come up with a foolproof plan to defeat him.

SIX

After breakfast the next morning, Tavarian and I met with the other council members in the circular chamber we'd designated as the council room when we'd first moved into the estate. Jallis, Rhia, Halldor, and several older dragon riders attended, along with Captain Ragorin, our infantry leader, and Petro Messei, the Warosian Admiral.

"So, both Zara and Lord Tavarian have made it back to us," Byron, one of the dragon rider lieutenants said. "This is good news! But you have brought two strange dragons with you, neither of whom seem to have riders. Who are they, and where did they come from?"

"Are you serious?" Halldor said. "*That's* the question you want to ask first?"

"I will tell you all the truth," Tavarian said. "But you must swear an oath that what I say will not leave this room. A *magically binding* oath," he added, as the other started to agree.

Byron scowled. "Now, that's hardly fair, Tavarian," he

protested. "You owe us an explanation!"

"I owe you nothing," he said. "And considering what I have done for our cause, I think I am worthy of a little trust at this point. If you can't give that to me, then this conversation is over."

A tense silence fell over the room. "It's fine," Daria said, volunteering herself as the voice of reason. "We'll do it."

Tavarian went around the table, performing the oath on each of them. It was a blood pact, sealed with a slice on each palm and a magical incantation. Tavarian had cast it on me, too, toward the beginning of our relationship, when he'd revealed to me that he was a mage. That vow had been a little more exten-sive than the one he was enacting now--he'd made me promise not to divulge *any* secret he told me without permission, not just one. Kind of annoying, but then I wasn't a tattletale anyway.

"Very well." Tavarian said once it was finished and settled back in his chair. He'd used his magic to heal the small cuts he'd made, and if not for the unnerved looks on the others' faces, I wouldn't have known anything had happened. At first I didn't understand why the others were so unsettled, and then I remembered that most people never saw magic performed outside of healings. To feel Tavarian's power rushing through them, binding them to their own words...they hadn't been prepared for it.

"Tell us, then," Byron said impatiently. "Where did these dragons come from?"

"Muza is my dragon," Tavarian said. There were shocked gasps, but Rhia, Jallis, and Halldor didn't seem surprised. "I sent him away after the conquest of Colitar, because he was heart-sick after being forced to kill so many people over a pointless war that was all about greed and had nothing to do with defending our country. I refused to put him through another battle like that, so I found a remote island for him to live on."

"You just left your dragon there, all by himself?" Byron asked, incredulous. "But it's been decades, Tavarian! How could you expect a dragon to live by himself on an island, without a single dragon or human for company?"

"Because he wasn't alone." Tavarian took a deep breath. "There were other dragons on the island, too."

A stunned silence fell over the room. Then, "Other dragons?" Ullion choked out. "You mean to tell us there's a whole island of abandoned dragons out there somewhere? Where are these riders who have left them behind, then?"

"Not abandoned dragons," Tavarian said. "*Free* dragons. They have never been bonded to a rider."

"That's impossible," Byron said flatly.

"It's not impossible," I butted in. "I went to the island myself, which is how I ended up bringing Serpol back here. He's one of the free dragons. His ancestors are amongst a handful of dragons who managed to flee the war entirely before Akron the Defender and his mages could bring them under their control. They were never subjected to the bonding spell."

"And you never thought to tell us about this, Tavarian?" Byron sputtered. "The dragon population has been declining for years! We could have bred these dragons with ours, used them to bring up our numbers!"

Tavarian slammed his fist on the table. "How dare you speak of them that way," he seethed, shocking the others--he very rarely displayed any sort of temper in public. "You are dragon riders, and you know better than anyone else that dragons are not simple beasts to be tamed. These free dragons are just like ours--intelligent and strong-willed, but also independent. They would have never risked mixing their bloodlines with our dragons and passing the bonding spell onto their young. They are *free*, and they will *remain* free."

Byron gave an exasperated huff. "You could have at least recruited them to help us with the war effort," he said.

"We *have*," I told him. "That's why Serpol is here."

"As if one dragon is going to make so much of a difference."

"He already has," Halldor snapped. "He and Muza helped our Commandant get back here safely. Which is more than can be said for *you*."

"All right, all right." Jallis held his palms up, taking on the role of peacemaker. "Enough arguing about this. It's not productive. Besides, we should be grateful that Tavarian and Muza arrived when they did. If they hadn't, some of us might not be sitting here today."

"It is fortuitous indeed that Muza arrived when he did, as Tavarian could not have used the horn aboard our ship without damaging it," the Admiral said. "But being angry at Tavarian for not recruiting all these dragons is foolish. Your defeat at the hands of the Zallabarians should have shown you that dragon warfare is becoming outdated. If you hope to continue defending your country after you've taken it back, you must start embracing modern warfare."

The rest of the council grumbled about this, but eventually they agreed with the admiral. Now that they were finally settled, Tavarian and I gave our reports, he about the Warosian alliance and his time studying with their mage scholar, and me about making it to the Hellmouth and destroying the piece of heart. The council was cheered by both, but especially by the success of my mission.

"What a relief!" Jallis exclaimed, clapping me on the shoulder. "It was bad enough that we had to deal with the Zallabarians--the last thing we needed was a battle with the dragon god on top of it."

"Does this really mean he's gone?" Daria demanded. "That he can never be resurrected?"

"As far as I know, yes." An uneasy feeling stirred in the pit of my stomach, but I brushed it aside. There was no way to bring the dragon god back without all five pieces of the heart--that was clear. I refused to spend any more time worrying about it when there were other things to discuss.

"What about Salcombe?" Rhia asked. "Do you think he survived?"

"There's a fifty-fifty chance," I admitted. "Most people wouldn't be able to survive their ship getting hit by a hurricane, but Salcombe is like a cockroach, and he did have the dragon god's power behind him." Truth be told, I wanted to consult Caor about it, see what he thought, but my divine mentor had been suspiciously absent these past few weeks. Was it because I'd been on the dragon archipelago? The gods didn't much like dragons, though Caor did seem to tolerate Lessie at least. I spun the tracking ring he'd given me around my forefinger, hoping he'd turn up soon.

"We'll worry about that when we have to," Tavarian said. "Now, can anyone tell me how the resistance effort is going?"

"Surprisingly well," Captain Ragorin said proudly. "The Zallabarians are distracted right now, which means our operatives have had more breathing room to hold meetings and recruit more resistance members."

"Distracted?" I asked. "How so?"

"As it turns out, too much victory can be a bad thing," Ragorin gave me a smug smile. "The Zallabarians have become over-confident, and as a result they have overextended themselves. In addition to holding Elantia, they now face three other enemies: the Warosians from the south, the Traggarans from the west--now that you and Tavarian have successfully botched that alliance--and then, to make matters worse, they have also attacked the Carrosians."

"The Carrosians? Really?" Rhia gaped. Carrosia was a vast country to the east, easily twice Zallabar's size. "That's madness!"

"It would seem that the autocrator has become too greedy," the Warosian admiral said thoughtfully. "Attacking on so many fronts means ever-lengthening supply lines. They must be severely stretched by this point."

"Exactly," Ragorin said. "Traggar is on the offensive now, constantly poaching both Zallabarian and Elantian colonies overseas, which of course Zallabar must defend. Zallabar is scrabbling to draft even more men for their occupation armies and to expand their navy with new ships, now that they no longer have the Traggaran navy to rely on as they'd planned."

"*New ships,*" Lessie said. "*Like the ones that tried to attack the dragon archipelago?*"

"*I guess so.*" I didn't say anything about that out loud though.

I didn't want to give the others any hint of the archipelago's location.

"Anyway, it is clear the Zallabarians simply do not have the resources or attention to hold onto everything they've grasped," Ragorin continued. "Which means this is the perfect time for us to strike. Their troops are all tied up at these other locations, so they cannot send more reinforcements if we launch an attack now."

"Not to mention that there's a lot of civil unrest in Elantia right now," Jallis put in. "Because of the lack of troops, the Zallabarians have been relying on older officers they've brought out of retirement--who, of course, aren't what they once were-- and local collaborators, who have quickly become despised by civilians. These collaborators are wealthy Elantians who have further enriched themselves by cooperating with the enemy, so naturally they are being reviled by the rest of the country."

"That is all well and good," the admiral said, "but what are our own numbers like? Do we have enough recruits from the resistance to augment our own forces? Even if the Zallabarians are 'overextended,' as you say, their armies are still many times greater than yours, and that was before so many of your soldiers were killed."

A ripple of resentment went through the room, and Captain Ragorin coughed. "We don't have as many recruits as we would like," he admitted. "Whether or not we succeed depends very much on the mood and reactions of the population and whether or not they will rally to our side. Many Elantians despise the dragon riders--half of them blame the dragons for their plight, and the other half think the riders have abandoned them."

"Well, that's hardly fair," Lessie protested angrily. *"The majority of the dragon force was kidnapped and held by the Zallabarians!"*

"Yes, but most people don't know that," I said gently, *"and the Zallabarians would have been quick to spread rumors that the dragon riders fled, if only to create more enmity and make it easier to turn the population to their side."*

"Very true," Tavarian went on. "Deserved or not, the population does not look very favorably upon dragon riders right now. With that in mind, I think Captain Ragorin should be the one to lead the attack."

"Ragorin?" Byron exclaimed. "But he is an infantry captain! Dragon riders have always led the attacks. It is tradition!"

"And where has tradition gotten us?" I demanded, pinning him with an angry gaze. The rider flinched but did not back down, squaring his shoulders instead. "Thanks to 'tradition', we're camping out on this forsaken island, refugees cast out of our own homes! If we want to win this war, we can't do things the 'traditional' way. We're going to have to think outside the box. I know you are part of the vanguard," I said, pinning Byron with a glare, "but if you want to get anything done, you'll need to let go of your pride and start working *with* us, not against us."

Byron's shoulders went rigid. "I don't mean to be difficult," he said stiffly. "It's just that this is...new for me."

"I'm pretty sure being kicked out of their own country is new to everyone here," Halldor said with a snort. "We're all struggling here, Byron."

"I agree that Ragorin should be the one to lead," Halldor said, "but what happens if we win? The old system was clearly a failure, so we can't go back to having only the sky-dwellers on the council."

"Agreed," Tavarian said. "We will need to form a new council, one where both ground-dwellers and sky-dwellers are fairly represented."

"I personally think we should get rid of those two classes altogether," Rhia said. "Class divisions serve only to further highlight our differences. And we need to get rid of the stigma behind dragon-rider and non-rider civilians fraternizing."

"What about the dragon-rider estates?" Jallis asked. "They were all taken over by the Zallabarians and their collaborators. Will they be given back to us?"

"They should be, wherever possible," Tavarian said. "After all, the families who built them have a prior claim. But rider privileges, such as tax exemptions, will be revoked."

We spent the rest of the meeting discussing potential new government systems, then broke for lunch. In the mess hall, I was a bit dismayed to see many of the dragon riders huddled in groups, away from the infantry, muttering amongst themselves. Word must have spread fast already, and more than a few cast resentful looks Ragorin's way.

"Hey." Ragorin nudged my shoulder, and he winked as I looked at him. "Don't worry about it. We infantry soldiers are used to getting spit on by riders. And, honestly, getting to lead the attack is a dream come true for us. If they want to cry about it, let 'em--it's just water off our backs."

"Maybe," I said, remembering Colonel Roche. She'd been in charge of the Traggaran Channel base, where I'd been stationed, and she had it in for me since day one thanks to her dragon rider prejudices. Because of her, I'd nearly been court-martialed out of the army, and I would have been if Tavarian hadn't shown up to save the day. The memory made me angry all over again, and before I realized what I was doing, I'd stood up and was marching over to one of the huddled groups.

"Hey." I stood over them, letting my shadow fall across the group.

The riders looked up at me, a mix of apprehension and resentment on their faces.

"What the hell is going on here? Why are you all forming cliques?" I cast my glance toward a group of non-riders, sitting ten feet away. "You guys usually all sit together."

"Yeah, well, that was before we found out that we might not be getting our family homes back," one of the riders said sullenly. "It's bad enough that my parents were killed in this forsaken war--now I'm going to be homeless, too?"

"Yeah, and what's this about having to pay taxes now?" another rider said. "Our families have been protecting Elantia for centuries, and now we've lost everything. We need to be able to rebuild without giving what little we have left back to the government!"

"Enough!" I stomped my foot, making their plates rattle. "I don't know where you heard this about not getting your homes back, but it's not true. If your homes haven't been burned to the ground by the enemy, then of course you'll be able to return to them. But, yes, you will have to start paying taxes and maybe find real work, too, since the enemy has probably looted your vaults. If we're going to rebuild and invest in better weapons, then everyone needs to start paying their fair share."

The riders grumbled about this, but the infantry soldiers seemed gratified. "You guys can sulk about this like toddlers if you want," I continued, "but we're still on the same side, and we're still fighting for the same thing. That means you're going to act like adults and sit together, not form stupid cliques like you're still in school."

I went around breaking up the groups, forcing the soldiers to co-mingle with each other once more. The riders were resistant, a few of them stomping out of the mess hall altogether, but most of them settled in, albeit reluctantly.

"They will get it over it," Tavarian said quietly when I finally joined him. "This is all a shock to them, first being ousted from their homes and now coming to terms with the fact that they will not be able to return to the privileged lives they once had even if they win the war."

"Well as far as I'm concerned, that's a good thing." I shrugged as I returned to my meal. It was our previous system and beliefs that had gotten us into so much trouble in the first place. If we wanted to survive, to rebuild our country and hold onto it, we had to let go of the past.

"Commandant!" A courier rushed into the mess hall, hair windblown and face flushed. The sullen atmosphere in the room dissipated in an instant, replaced with taut anticipation, and my own heartbeat sped up. He skidded to a halt in front of me and snapped a quick salute. "I bring urgent news."

"From where?" I demanded.

"Zuar City." He grinned. "The autocrator is coming to the capital. This is our chance to bring him down."

SEVEN

"**A**utocrator Reichstein is coming to Zuar City?" I asked, startled at the news. "I didn't think he would be paying a visit to Elantia so soon. Isn't he overextended right now?"

"His armies are," Tavarian agreed. "Which is likely why Reichstein has decided to visit the capital. To remind us who is in charge."

"Exactly." The courier handed me a letter. "This is from Lieutenant Diran."

Right. The spy we'd stationed in Zuar City. I unfolded the envelope, and Tavarian and I read the contents together. The entire mess hall was silent, as if everyone was waiting with bated breath for me to read the letter aloud.

"Well?" Jallis demanded. "What does it say?"

"Council chamber," I said abruptly, rising from my seat. "Now."

The council members followed me into the chamber, and

Halldor closed the door firmly behind us. "The lieutenant says that Reichstein will be in the capital in four days," I told them as we settled around the table. "Reichstein will be accompanied by his highest staff, which means there will be some very high-value targets. Not to mention the autocrator himself. This is the perfect time to take him out."

"They will have very stiff security for such an event," Byron pointed out. "Are we certain that organizing an assassination attempt against him now is the right thing to do?"

"While it's true he will have security, he will not be nearly as well protected as he is in Zallabar," Kade pointed out. "We have a growing Resistance who are willing to help us, and a solid spy network established across the country."

"Taking out the autocrator will make all the difference," Tavarian added. "The entire country will be thrown into confusion, which will make it easier for us to strike back. The Zallabarians might even withdraw entirely, since they are spread so thin right now."

"Very well," Byron said. "But who will we send on such an important mission? We cannot send just anybody to complete the task."

"I'll go," I said before anyone else could volunteer. "I've spent quite a bit of time amongst the Zallabarians, and I've actually met the autocrator, so I know what he looks like."

"Then I will go with you," Tavarian said.

"Who are you leaving in charge?" Rhia asked. "Jallis again?"

"It really should be Captain Ragorin," Jallis pointed out, nodding at the captain as he spoke. "He and his men have been the ones whipping this place into shape."

"Agreed," I said. I was really impressed with how much more organized the base was since I'd left. "Ragorin will be in charge." I side-eyed the older riders, who begrudgingly nodded. I knew they hadn't been happy with letting younger upstarts like Rhia and Jallis run things, and they wouldn't be pleased about a non-rider taking charge, either, but the fact was that most of the riders didn't have experience running an army. They were about as spoiled as a member of the military could be. "But only until it's time for him to lead the attack," I added. "Byron will be in charge of the base then."

Byron seemed surprised, but gratified. "You won't want me on the front lines, Commandant?"

I shook my head. "A few of the dragon riders need to stay behind to guard the island. You'll be one of them."

We spent the rest of the meeting hashing out the details of both the assassination and the impending attack. Muza and Lessie would take Tavarian and me to Zuar City, and Rhia and Halldor would accompany us for part of the journey before splitting off to carry out a mission of their own: destroying an important depot and enemy camp. Captain Ragorin would send units back to the mainland and into the major cities and ports with orders to go active as soon as news of the autocrator's death came in, to help our spies foment rebellion and to aid in overthrowing the local military as needed. The Warosian admiral agreed to ferry arms to the rebels via the ports, by night.

"May I accompany you?" Serpol asked me as we were wrapping up, and I startled. I wasn't used to anyone other than Lessie intruding upon my thoughts. *"My magic will prove quite useful, and I would like to see Elantia properly."*

"Of course." Serpol's abilities would allow us to communicate more freely with one another, and his shielding and invisibility spells combined with Tavarian's magic would make this trip a breeze.

"Maybe we can take out some enemy camps on our way in," Lessie said eagerly. *"I've been eager to barbecue some Zallabarians."*

"Maybe," I replied, reluctantly amused. Unlike Muza, who was a pacifist, Lessie was bloodthirsty by nature, always up for wreaking havoc against the enemy. *"But not too many. We have to stay focused on our objective."*

"Objective, obschmective." I could practically see her rolling her eyes. *"With all this doom and gloom, we still have to remember to have a little fun every once in a while."*

I held back a snort. *"You and I have very different ideas of 'fun'."*

With the meeting finished, I headed back to my tower room to pack my things while Tavarian went to give instructions to the airship crew for the time of our absence. We'd be leaving tomorrow, bright and early, so we could get into the city well before the autocrator arrived. I pulled out my travel pack, emptied it, and sorted through the items I wanted to take and the ones I wanted to leave behind. Once I was satisfied, I repacked, adding several changes of clothes, then grabbed a sharpening stone, sat down on my bed, and began sharpening my knives. My dragon blade stayed in its sheath strapped to my leg--the weapon was forged by mages, and never seemed to need sharpening no matter how many times I used it.

A sound rustled behind me, and I whirled, the knife I was sharpening clutched in one fist.

Caor, standing by the window, quirked an eyebrow. "Go ahead," he said, an amused smile on his handsome face. The breeze coming in through the window gently tousled his long brown hair, and he crossed his muscular arms over his bare chest. "See if you can actually stab me with that."

"Yeah, right." Rolling my eyes, I set the knife down on the bed. Despite looking completely solid, Caor was only semi-corporeal--the blade would pass through him as if he didn't exist. "Nice of you to show up. I've been trying to summon you for weeks."

"Sorry." He shrugged one well-defined shoulder. "I've been busy in the other realm. You threw us into quite a tizzy when you gave Derynnis the second piece of heart to keep for himself." He chuckled. "Not everyone is happy about that decision."

"Yeah, well, then maybe they should have bargained with Derynnis instead." Giving him the second piece was the only way to get him to destroy the first, ensuring that the dragon god could never be resurrected. "This is what happens when you send a mortal to do your dirty work."

"Indeed." Caor gave me a dry look. "You know, you act as if you were doing the gods a favor, when in reality if you hadn't--"

"I know, I know." Of course I'd destroyed the heart to save humanity's hide. "But you guys don't have to act so ungrateful about it." After all, the gods' existence depended on ours, and if Zakyiar destroyed us they would cease to be. "Anyway, what's going on? Are you here to congratulate me, finally? Or are you bringing me another problem?"

Caor scoffed. "I'm here to warn you, actually." He took a step forward, his typically mischievous expression turning grave. "Salcombe survived the hurricane that you and your dragon set upon him--a very nice touch, by the way, using your dragon's fire and momentum like that. Not sure I would have thought of it."

"Thanks," I said, dread dropping into the pit of my stomach. I'd known in my heart that Salcombe had survived, but hearing it spoken aloud by Caor made it all too real. "Any idea where he is? What he's planning next?"

"He is in Zallabar, at the capital, but I do not know what he is up to precisely," Caor said. "He seems to have retained the power in the pieces of heart he possesses and is using the dragon god's magic to shield his activities from me. But I do know that he is coming for you, Zara. He seeks vengeance against you for destroying what he considers his life's work."

"You mean for saving his ass and everyone else's," I muttered. I held no illusions about the dragon god--he was known as the World Eater, a being of immense power that went from planet to planet, dimension to dimension, consuming all the resources of one place before moving onto the next. He would have swallowed Salcombe whole once he'd returned, since he would have had no use for him. But, of course, Salcombe hadn't wanted to see that truth. He'd been a dying man, slowly wasting away because of illness, and the dragon god's power had given him a new chance at life. Of course he wasn't going to look upon Zakyiar as anything but his savior.

"If you are looking for gratitude from that man, you will be looking for a very long time," Caor said, amused once more. "Truly though, Zara, you must be very careful. Salcombe is out making powerful allies right now, using his power and influence to manipulate them into doing his bidding. And even though the dragon god cannot be resurrected, Salcombe still has more than half of his heart. Zakyiar still has the potential to wreak havoc on this world."

A chill raced down my spine. "What are you talking about? You said the dragon god would be vanquished once I destroyed the piece of heart."

"I said he couldn't be resurrected," Caor said sternly. "But with so much of his heart still left intact--not to mention that there is a fourth piece still in existence, though thankfully not on this plane--there is a chance he could come back. If the dragon-god cult Salcombe created manages to spread their religion to the masses and reel in millions of faithful adherents, the dragon god could easily use their adoration to manifest in semi-corporeal form. Until you destroy Salcombe and discredit his cult, your mission is not truly over."

"Dammit!" I slammed the side of my fist against the wall. *Just when I thought I could finally focus on the war, Caor blindsides me with this?* "You know, it would have been really nice if you'd told me this from the beginning," I snapped. "I would have tried to get Salcombe's other pieces away from him sooner."

"And risked your own pieces in the process," Caor said. "No, it was better that you focused on the goal. Zakyiar returning in his fully realized form would have been infinitely worse."

I sighed, leaning against the wall. "So what do you suggest I do? Send my men to root out Salcombe's cultists?" I wondered if his acolytes still met in the catacombs below Zuar City, or if they'd found another place to perform their creepy rituals. But then again, was Zuar City the only place they were located? What if he'd established sects all over the country? Salcombe was well-traveled, after all, and had residences all over Elantia and other countries besides.

"Be on your guard," Caor suggested. "Salcombe will come for you, and his eyes and ears will certainly report to him if you show up in Zuar City, which is a much easier location for him to attack you than this remote, well-defended island."

"Wonderful," I muttered. I was always on my guard, but Salcombe wasn't exactly easy to watch out for. With the power of the dragon god and the face-changing fan he'd stolen from me, he could readily assume different disguises and cloak his presence from me.

Caor seemed to read my thoughts, for he added, "I will keep an eye turned toward Salcombe at all times and will alert you if he draws close. Though the rest of the gods will not interfere, I recognize what you have done for us. You will always have a friend in me."

"Thank you." I was surprised at the sincerity in his words, and tears stung at the corners of my eyes. "That means a lot to me. I'd hug you if I could."

Caor laughed, closing the distance between us. "You can," he said, his arms coming around me. "But only for a moment."

I hesitated, then embraced him, sliding my arms around his torso to rest my hands against his bare back. He circled his arms around my waist, and I leaned in, marveling at how solid he felt, at the fact that there was actually something to lean *on*. This close, I could smell his scent, something sweet and herbal but light. Faint golden light emanated from his skin, tiny sparkles skipping along his flesh and humming with power, and I was awe-struck for a second as I realized I was basking in his divine glow.

And just like that, he vanished around me.

"Can't let you do that for too long." His laughter echoed throughout the room, and my cheeks burned as I realized I'd let myself slip into some kind of trance. "We gods tend to have a hypnotic effect on humans. Probably has something to do with the fact that we created you and can bend you to our will."

"But only in person, apparently," I called back sarcastically. "Maybe you guys should consider visiting more often if you don't want us running amuck and getting into trouble."

Caor didn't answer that, but he didn't have to. I knew his reply would be something along the lines of "but where's the fun in that?" and now that I'd spent enough time around him, I was starting to understand it. The gods created us for entertainment. They would nudge things here and there and occasionally respond to our requests and offerings, but for the most part they wanted to sit back and watch us do the work. If they interfered too much, they'd be investing too much of themselves into our lives. They would become *responsible*.

And now that the gods were holding a grudge against humanity, the only time they would step in was to save their own hides.

I finished sharpening my knives, then went down to the fields to spend some time with Lessie. She was out there with the other dragons, sunning herself, but she lifted her great head as I approached, her fiery eyes lighting up.

Sighing, I laid my cheek against hers, letting her warmth soak into me.

"*Is everything okay?*" she asked, sensing my distress.

"I'm just tired." Which was perfectly true. I was so damn tired. Of the war, of Salcombe, of the dragon god, of everything. But I didn't want to tell her about Caor's visit, not yet. That would be a conversation for tomorrow, when everyone was present.

"*Well, the only cure for tiredness is a good nap,*" Lessie declared. Lying back down in the grass, she used one of her clawed hands to gently pull me in against her belly. "*Relax, Zara. There will be plenty of time to stress about things tomorrow. This time is for preparing, for gathering our energy so we can barbecue Zallabarians tomorrow.*"

I laughed, snuggling against Lessie's side. "One barbecue, coming right up." Maybe, on our way in, we would raid a few camps tomorrow after all. The more chaos we could stir up, the better.

EIGHT

The next morning, we left with the dawn, the golden pink haze brightening the horizon as we flew east, heading toward the mainland. As we traveled, I told Tavarian, Rhia, Halldor, and the dragons about Caor's visit, and the dire news he'd brought.

"Are you serious?" Halldor yelled, and I winced as his too-loud voice stabbed into my ear via the magical earpieces we used to communicate. "Sorry," he said, correctly reading the look of pain on my face. "I didn't mean to shout. But dragon's balls, this is too much. I thought we'd put this dragon-god thing behind us!"

"There's always something," Rhia said, a little forlornly. But when I glanced at her, she straightened her shoulders. "Still, Zara, we've survived everything Salcombe and the dragon god have thrown at us so far. We're not going to let him get to us now that we're so close to ending this war."

"I wish Caor had been able to tell us more," Tavarian said,

his brow furrowed in frustration. "But without knowing exactly where Salcombe is and who these allies are, there really isn't anything we can do. Especially if he isn't in Elantia. We simply don't have enough time or resources to go after him while also taking out the autocrator."

"True." I bit my lip, thinking more about Caor's warning. "I guess it's not like we have to go after him right now. He can't recruit masses of followers overnight to worship the dragon god and help him manifest."

"Who would be stupid enough to worship a god like Zakyiar anyway?" Halldor wondered aloud. "Salcombe and his acolytes would have to lie about his true nature. No one would support a god if they knew his sole purpose for being here was to devour their world."

"Merely bending the truth would be sufficient," Tavarian pointed out. "Just as Salcombe believes he is exempt from the dragon god's greed, so do his acolytes. Besides, people have had a fascination with death and chaos since the beginning of time. There are primitive cultures out there whose entire societies are built around worshipping death gods. Not to mention others who are resentful of bigger nations like Elantia and Zallabar and who are willing to embrace any sort of perverted gospel if it means bringing down their enemies."

A heavy silence fell over us as the others contemplated this possibility. "Well, at least we don't have to worry about the dragon god attacking us in our dreams anymore," I said, trying to dispel the grim mood.

"True," Rhia said with a shudder. "It was pretty awful, the way he was constantly accosting us in our nightmares."

Our discussion turned toward Rhia and Halldor's upcoming mission—tomorrow, they would be splitting off from us, heading east toward the munitions depot. "I wish that we could do something like that too," Lessie groused. "It doesn't seem fair that they get to engage the enemy while we're stuck hiding outside the capital waiting for you and Tavarian."

"Perhaps there is a mission that we might be able to complete as well?" Serpol suggested.

"Actually, there is a large munitions depot in the main military camp outside the capital," Rhia said. "You, Muza, and Serpol could destroy it. The fewer weapons the enemy has access to, the better chance we have when our army finally attacks."

"I like that idea," Lessie said to me, perking up.

"You'll have to be careful," I warned. "You should scout the place first, get as much intel as you can before you do anything."

"Of course," Serpol said. "We'll do so at night, and I'll use my magic to shield us so we can approach undetected."

We camped together that night in the forest, and the next morning, Rhia and Halldor took off. Tavarian and I continued on, with Serpol flying alongside us. The clouds were fairly thick, and the air frigid, and I was forced to put on extra layers over my dragon-rider armor, even with Lessie's warmth.

"I'll be glad when we arrive," she said, shivering a little. "This is cold even for me."

As we drew closer to Zuar City and our impending mission, I started to wonder if we were doing the right thing. I felt a little odd about the idea of killing the autocrator--I'd met him in person at a party in the Zallabarian capital, and he'd been quite likable, even humble.

"Yes, but he is still the enemy," Tavarian said when I voiced the thought aloud. "How many dragons and men, both Elantian and Zallabarian, have died to satisfy his ambition? How many more will die still if he isn't stopped?"

"You're right." I sighed, scraping a hand through my curls. "It's just...is it dishonorable, killing him this way? With no chance at all to fight back?" I was being silly, I knew--I'd never fought fair in my life. But although I'd killed in battle, in self-defense, and to protect my loved ones, I'd never killed someone in cold blood like this.

"Not at all," Tavarian said. "He is not a civilian, and it isn't as if there ever will be an opportunity to meet him on the battle-field. The autocrator has tens of thousands of men to do the fighting for him; he would never engage directly. Besides, even getting to him is going to be quite a challenge. The risk of us being caught and killed is very high."

"*A risk that is well worth it,*" Lessie put in. "*If these warmonger politicians were killed more often, rather than being allowed to hide behind the shield of their soldiers, they might think twice before starting wars of aggression.*"

"Have you ever used magic to kill anyone before?" I asked Tavarian. We had already agreed beforehand that we wouldn't use a weapon--it would be too easy to get caught, and we'd have to get too close for comfort. Instead, we would use a death spell, one Tavarian had learned during his time in Warosia.

"Apart from the horn, no," Tavarian admitted. "While I know the death spell in theory, I haven't used it on a human before. To be honest, I am not even certain what kind of range it has."

Muza snorted at that.

"We can't go into the capital without knowing the limitations of the spell," Lessie protested. *"He is going to have to practice before then."*

We flew for a few more hours before finally landing in a thickly wooded forest just outside the underground palace I'd discovered years ago on a treasure hunt. The dragons would drop us off at the capital the next day, then scout the encampment. They had agreed to hide out in the underground palace when they weren't doing reconnaissance and not to attack without telling us what they'd found first.

We set up camp inside the palace, in the great hall I'd discovered the first time I found this place. "This is a great hideout," Tavarian said, craning his neck to look around. Statues set into arched recesses looked down on us from their stern noses as we ate on the dirty marble floor, our campfire casting harsh shadows on their alabaster faces. "We can light fires down here without giving away our position."

"Exactly." I leaned against Lessie, who was curled up behind me. Muza was on Tavarian's other side, while Serpol stood guard, invisible, outside. He would alert us if anyone approached.

My treasure sense pinged continuously as I ate, and even though I'd turned down the volume, it still nagged at me. "There are so many amazing artifacts here," I said, sighing wistfully. "Ones that I haven't been able to carry off because they're just too heavy."

"We'll come back after we win the war," Tavarian promised. He chewed thoughtfully on a piece of apple, the firelight dancing in his mercurial eyes as he stared at me. "Is your plan to go back to treasure hunting after things settle down?"

"I'd like to," I admitted. The thought of things returning to the way they were, of running the shop with Carina, of exploring the world and excavating long-forgotten sites for treasure, sounded like a dream come true.

But could things really go back to the way they were? I wasn't the same old treasure hunter--I had a dragon in my life now, not to mention a fiancé, and I was one of the leaders of a rag-tag army. I'd never enjoy the same anonymity I once had as an orphan turned treasure hunter, a ground dweller who'd never been of notice or importance to anyone. Would I be expected to help run things? Certainly I wanted to make sure the new government we established was one that was just and fair for all, but what about after that? Would I sit on the council? How much of my time would that take up?

Tavarian seemed to read my thoughts, for he placed his hand over mine. "We'll make time for your treasure hunting," he said softly. "No matter what."

A lump swelled in my throat. "Thank you." I knew it was silly, this attachment to an occupation that was so dangerous, but I couldn't help it. Treasure hunting was in my blood; it was as much a part of me as dragon riding.

We sat in silence a while longer, contemplating the future as we ate. We'd nearly finished when Tavarian pointed at one of the statues on the wall. "Say, isn't that Caor?"

My head shot up, and I stared in the direction Tavarian had

pointed. Sure enough, the statue staring back at me was a larger-than-life replica of the messenger god, complete with his messenger bag, kilt, winged sandals, and trademark grin. Horns curved over his long hair, but aside from that, the depiction was startlingly faithful.

"Actually," Caor said from behind me, "I do sometimes show the horns."

I twisted to see him standing just in the shadows, his grin glinting in the dark. He stepped into view, and my mouth dropped open at the sight of the curling ram horns, each one twice as thick as my fist. "They're a bit heavy though, so I usually do without. Gives me headaches sometimes."

"I can imagine," I said dryly.

Caor snapped his fingers, and the horns disappeared. He sat down right next to Tavarian, who seemed a little startled, and grinned at him. "Nice to see you again. You know, I never got to tell you this, but you look a bit like the champion we sent to defend humanity all those years ago."

"I do?" Tavarian was taken aback.

Caor nodded. "It's mostly in the eyes." He peered into Tavarian's face. "Those silvery irises you got. Rare color, you know, and back then children born with those eyes were considered messengers of the gods. But there's something about your jawline, too, and the way you carry yourself."

"I suppose I'll take that as a compliment," Tavarian said in a strangled voice.

I hid a grin as I watched them, secretly enjoying seeing Tavarian thrown so off balance. I'd never seen him this flustered before, and I was delighted to know he wasn't always so perfect.

"If Tavarian has messenger eyes, then why was I chosen as the champion instead?" I butted in.

Caor glanced at me with a shrug. "Guess the others figured we should try a different bloodline. Though it's not like your beloved here hasn't played his part." He gave Tavarian a sly look that made me nervous.

"Are you going to tell us what you came here for?" I asked as Caor plucked an apple from our bag of reserves. "Or are you just here to eat our food?"

"What, a god can't come hang out with his favorite mortal?" Caor sounded wounded, though he ruined the effect somewhat by biting into the apple with a loud crunch. "Now that you mention it, though, I did want to warn you that Salcombe and the dragon god have been communing quite a bit. They're definitely planning something."

My meal soured in my stomach. "Is he coming to Zuar City?"

"Maybe. But he's not anywhere near the capital right now."

I let out a sigh of relief.

"Good," Tavarian said. "If he's not nearby then he won't interfere with our plans."

"I wouldn't be so sure of that," Caor warned. "Salcombe might not do anything directly, but he has acolytes in the city who worship the dragon god. Zakyiar is devious and extremely motivated right now. Be on your guard."

He vanished, taking the apple with him.

"Wonderful," I sighed, pitching the remnants of my own apple into the fire. "Another thing to worry about."

"There is always something to worry about," Tavarian

pointed out. "But try not to worry too much, Zara. It does no good, and we need to focus on the mission."

"True." I wiped my hands and stood up. "Let's go up top and test this spell of yours out. Does it work on plants and animals?"

"On anything living," Tavarian confirmed. He pulled a small notebook from his pocket and riffled through it. "I have all the spells I learned written down here."

I got to my feet, then went over and grasped the thick rope we'd left dangling from the hole in the ceiling. "Serpol, a little help?" I called.

I heard a rumble of movement as Serpol grasped the rope, then gently lifted me out of the hole. A wave of vertigo swept through me as I briefly dangled high in the air before being deposited on the ground. I watched as Serpol pulled Tavarian up as well, a little amused as he floated into the air and then on the ground—since Serpol was still invisible, it looked as though Tavarian had flown out of the hole of his own accord.

"Thank you." Tavarian patted Serpol's hide, then opened up his notebook. He briefly reviewed the spell, and then we moved into the woods, well away from the dragons.

"Let's try plants first," I suggested. "How about that bush over there?" I pointed to a shrub a few feet away.

Tavarian nodded, his expression grim. He raised his hands, chanting quietly in a strange, guttural language. A sudden wind picked up, and power crackled in the air, solidifying around his hands like purple lightning. His face tightened with concentration as he fought to control the energy, and then he pointed at the bush with his left hand.

A stream of energy shot out of the tip of his finger and into the bush. The effect was instantaneous: the bush briefly lit up, then withered, the leaves falling away and disintegrating to ash, the branches curling and twisting until they were dead, dried out husks. The stiff wind blew it all away, scattering the ashes across the forest, leaving not so much as a single root behind.

In the span of a few seconds, the bush ceased to be.

"Damn." I stared at the spot where the shrub had been, my skin clammy. "That was...very final. Is that what's going to happen to the autocrator? He'll turn into a pile of dust and disappear?"

"Essentially, yes," Tavarian said. "I practiced on a few rats the first time I did this, so I've seen the effect before." He gave me a sidelong look. "It was quite unsettling for me, too."

So I wasn't the only one creeped out. "Let's see exactly how much range and finesse we've got with this thing."

Tavarian and I spent an hour practicing using larger and smaller targets and varying the distances. We discovered he could shoot the spell accurately up to fifty yards, and could also target small and large life forms. We tried hitting a small tree branch once, just to see if he could kill only the branch, but the entire tree withered and died on the spot. The reality of how dangerous this spell was chilled me to the bone. If it even grazed your pinky finger, you'd be dead.

Tavarian wiped at the sheen of sweat on his face and leaned against a tree trunk. "Okay," he said, sliding to the ground. "I need a break."

"That one took a lot out of you, huh?" I said, offering him a piece of jerky. Each time he performed the spell, he grew more tired, and the larger the object, the more draining it was.

He nodded, gratefully accepting the snack. "That tree was quite large, so yes."

We were just about to get up when something rustled in the distance, followed by a threatening snort.

"A boar," Tavarian breathed, going still.

A pair of large tusks poked out from behind a bush, and the animal pushed its way through the undergrowth, pawing at the ground.

"Shit." I drew my dragon blade, prepared to gore the animal. What was it with boars and me? This was the second time I'd been attacked by one in as many weeks!

The boar charged, but before it could make it even a few feet, Tavarian blasted it with the death spell. The boar disintegrated mid-run, its ashes blowing everywhere, and I threw a hand up over my face, coughing as I accidentally inhaled some. It tasted awful, bitter and thick and grainy on my tongue, and I sputtered, reaching for the water flask at my hip.

"That's it." Tavarian panted, looking paler than usual, his eyelids heavy. He leaned his head against the tree trunk. "I am done for the night."

I helped Tavarian back to the underground palace, where he fell asleep almost immediately. As he snored softly, the two of us snuggled in while the dragons slept, I stared up at the ceiling, brooding over the implications of what we'd learned. Using the spell on the boar had taken a lot out of him—even more so than the tree. Would he faint if he used it on the autocrator and it took too much out of him?

Don't be silly, I chided myself. Tavarian had nearly passed out, yes, but that was after an hour of practice. He would be refreshed and ready when it came time to face the autocrator. I just hoped he didn't miss and accidentally hit anyone else, because we'd only have two or three shots before he burned out completely.

That's what back up plans are for, I told myself. I pulled a small glass perfume bottle from my pocket and held it up. The tiny bit of moonlight filtering into the tent glinted off the polished glass. It was too dark to see the liquid, but I knew it was a lurid green--a special poison derived from the juice of a tiny mushroom. If I could get close enough to spritz this at the autocrator, he would be dead within minutes.

But that was a last resort, to be used only if Tavarian didn't have a clear shot. If Tavarian used the spell and failed, there would be no opportunity to get close to the autocrator. Because the two of us would be dead.

NINE

The next morning, the dragons took us to Zuar City. Serpol used his magic to keep us hidden as we soared through the sky in broad daylight, and we set down in Briarwood Forest, just ten miles away from the west gate. A shiver raced through me I scanned the familiar trees—the last time I'd been here, on what was supposed to be a stealth training exercise, we'd been attacked by a Zallabarian airship, and Ulllion had nearly lost his dragon. Zara and I had managed to bring it down with Rhia and Ykos's help, but the show of force had been terrifying, our first glimpse of what the Zallabarians were truly capable of.

"Be careful, Lessie," I said as I hugged her goodbye. "Remember, reconnaissance only. No barbecuing until we give the go-ahead."

"*Spoilsport,*" she huffed affectionately. "*I'm the one who should be telling you to be careful. You're about to go into the enemy's lair, and you don't even have dragon hide to protect you.*"

"I guess we'll both have to be careful, then," I said lightly, trying not to let my doubts crowd in. I'd spent enough time last night thinking of all the ways this could go wrong--now was the time for action.

Serpol flapped his wings, and the three dragons shimmered out of existence, cloaked by his magic. As they took flight, the wind from their wings kicked up dust into our faces, forcing me to shield my eyes. Apparently Serpol's spell didn't hide their presence completely--I wondered what an airship crew would think if they saw a bird fly into one of the dragons, splatting against a huge, invisible beast. They would probably be baffled. The ridiculous thought made me smile.

"We should disguise ourselves now," Tavarian said. "Did you pack your change of clothes?"

"Yes." I pulled a simple blue dress and bonnet out of my bag. My boots--spelled to hide the sound of my footfalls--would stay on, but the dress was long enough to hide them, and it had a specially stitched pocket in the skirt to tuck my dragon blade into. I pulled on the outfit while Tavarian changed into trousers, a red-and-white checkered shirt, and a navy blue vest. A pair of round spectacles went onto his nose, and he used his magic to alter his face, softening his angular features to make himself appear more ordinary and dulling his arresting silver eyes to a faded, unassuming blue.

"Your turn," he said, cupping my face in his hands.

My cheeks tingled as his magic worked its way into my skin, and I watched in the reflection of his eyes as he made my nose and cheeks rounder, my lips thinner, my skin darker. My eyes became dark brown and slanted, and the stray curls peeking out from beneath my bonnet turned coal black.

"Huh." I pursed my lips as I studied my new look. "I kinda like it." I couldn't have looked more different, but there was something appealing about that. Like I was reinventing myself.

"Good." Tavarian pecked my forehead, then took my hand in his. "Now let's go. We have a lot to do."

We set out on foot, hand in hand, with our packs slung across our shoulders like a married couple on a journey. Which, in a way, we were--not married yet, although perhaps we soon would be, but we *were* a couple on a journey. We walked for about an hour, discussing our plans for the day, then stopped in a village where we changed into more respectable clothing and hired a carriage to take us the rest of the way.

Like last time, there were guards stationed at each gate, screening the entrants. I noticed that this time there were two lines: One was made up of merchants, driving carts or traveling with donkeys, entering the city to sell their wares. They were regulars who already had passes, and were waved in quickly. The second line, which we stood in, was made up of travelers planning to visit friends or family or here for business.

"Names?" the guard asked as we rolled up.

Tavarian poked his head out the window. He looked down at the guard with such an air of superiority that I had to choke back a laugh. "Mr. and Mrs. Brighton," he said in a snooty voice. "My wife and I have traveled all the way from Littington after hearing that the dragon rider estates are being sold off. We hope to acquire some new pieces for our home."

"You're collectors, then?" the guard said. He took in Tavarian's velvet hat and the gold watch chain hanging from his waistcoat pocket, no doubt deciding whether or not we were wealthy enough to travel all this way just for some antiques. He scribbled something on the pad he was carrying, then handed us a sheet of paper. "You'll need a trading pass, then. This'll last you a week."

"A week is sufficient." Tavarian tucked the pass into his pocket, then turned away, clearly dismissing the man.

I wondered whether it was wise to provoke the guard in this way, but the man let us through without incident, though he was a bit grumpy about it.

"Guards are used to entitled toffs treating them like the help," Tavarian said, reading the look on my face. "It would have been more suspicious if I'd been deferential."

"Right." The affluent customers who came into the Treasure Trove acted the same way, expecting to be waited on hand and foot. And, of course, Carina and I put up with it because we wanted the money. I imagined the guards had been told to let all traders through; the city needed all the gold it could get, since the occupation was putting a crimp in the nation's economy. People were a lot less likely to travel and spend their money when there were Zallabarian guards everywhere, watching for even the slightest hint of suspicious behavior. That kind of atmosphere really put a damper on vacations.

Though I desperately wanted to see Carina and our shop, we traveled straight to Dragon's Table instead, where we booked a room at an exclusive hotel known to be frequented by Zallabarian officers and officials. Tavarian and I had packed a small fortune's worth of gold to help solidify our cover as wealthy merchants, so the suite we were shown into was lavish, with plush furnishings and priceless artwork decorating each room, a large four-poster bed, and a bathtub big enough to fit four people with room to spare.

"I wondered what they'd done with the dragon rider academy," I said softly as I stared out the tall window in the suite's living room. I could see the academy from here, and my heart twisted at the sight of Zallabarian flags flying from its towers and turrets instead of the dragon rider family emblems. Memories rose in my head--of Lessie's first flight, of Major Falkieth's warfare lessons, of time spent in the stables, of long walks with Rhia and exciting adventures with Jallis. It felt like another lifetime ago.

"At least they haven't torn it down," Tavarian said, coming to stand behind me. The Zallabarians had turned the academy into a barracks for the soldiers, who were out doing drills in the fields. I wondered how the Zallabiaran soldiers felt, practicing in the very spot our dragons had once used as a playground. There would still be huge prints left in the ground from dragons running and playing. Not to mention dragon dung, some of which was gigantic, depending on the size of the dragon. As cadets, we'd had to clean the field every week, and I smirked at the thought of the Zallabarians being forced to do it when they moved in.

Tavarian and I washed up, then went downstairs to the hotel's restaurant for lunch. As we waited for our food to arrive, Tavarian leaned across the table and slid his hand into my hair, a tender look in his eye. I might have thought he was simply being romantic, if not for the sparks of magic pricking at my ear.

A second later, the background noise came sharply into focus, and my eyes widened as the vague buzz of sound turned into real conversations.

"What do you mean, you are out of lobster bisque?" a woman complained to the waiter. She sounded like she was right next to me, but when I craned my neck, tracing the sound, I saw she was five tables away.

"Get this salad out to table nine!" I heard someone else say from all the way in the kitchen. The voice was quickly swept away in the tide of other conversations. Overwhelmed, I resisted the urge to clap my hand over my ears.

Tavarian took my hand in his. "A hearing-amplification spell," he said. "I know it seems like you're being bombarded with sound right now, but you can control it. Just pick one conversation and focus in on it. The others will fade out as you follow the trail of sound."

The waiter brought us our soup, and I did as Tavarian said while eating spoonfuls of seafood chowder, picking one conversation thread at a time, deciding whether it was worth listening to, then moving onto the next.

"I have to say that this Elantian food is getting tiresome," a captain was saying. "I miss my wife's home cooking."

"Why don't you bring her out here?" the other officer asked. "We're stuck here for at least a year. If I had a wife at home, especially one who could cook, I'd have brought her out here first thing."

"I thought about it," the captain said, "but I don't like the mood of the city right now. The Elantians are growing more and more restive, bucking against authority, ignoring curfews, hosting secret meetings. You'd think we would have beaten them into submission by now."

"They are a stubborn people and not used to being on the losing side," the other officer said. "It will take them time to accept their defeat."

"Yes, well, in the meantime I don't feel safe bringing my wife out here," the captain grumbled. "She's safe back home, with her family, so she'll stay there unless the situation changes. I'll just have to put in a request for leave in a few months. Don't want her to forget she's still married."

"That's an odd way of saying that you want to see her because you miss her," the officer said, sounding amused. "Still, it isn't so bad here. After all, the autocrator is coming to visit, isn't he? He wouldn't come if he didn't think it was safe."

"The autocrator will have a personal army guarding him at all times," the captain said. "Of course it'll be safe, for him."

We listened for another hour, but didn't hear anything of note. The officers in general seemed very tense about the autocrator's visit and determined to protect him at all costs. Rumors of rebellion were swirling around in the streets. Not great for us, since it was putting them all on edge.

But at least it meant the spies and recruiters we'd planted were doing their jobs.

After lunch, Tavarian went out to scout the most likely venues for the autocrator's visit, since no one knew exactly where he'd be staying yet. Feeling tired, I retreated to the suite and lay down for a much-needed nap.

I was just nodding off when a sharp knock at the door startled me awake. I bolted upright, my hand slipping beneath the pillow next to me, where I'd tucked away my dragonblade. "Who is it?" I called.

The door flew open, and two Zallabarian soldiers marched in.

"Why I never!" I scolded, using my best scandalized tone as I jumped to my feet. My heart rate sped up as they pinned me with identical, narrow-eyed stares, taking in my rumpled hair and the simple shift I'd stripped down to sleep in. "How dare you barge into my room like this!"

"Sorry, ma'am," the guard on the left said, though he didn't sound sorry at all. He was a strawberry blond, while his partner was a brunette with a hooked nose. "The governor has ordered us to check into all hotel guests. Where is your husband?"

"Out shopping," I said stiffly. "I planned to join him, but I was feeling under the weather, as you can see."

"We'll have to come back and speak to him separately, then," Hooked Nose said. "Where is your permit?"

I produced it for them, and the guards were silent for a minute as they studied it. "A trade permit?" Strawberry Blond asked. "For what?"

"My husband and I are merchants," I explained. "We have a special fondness for antiquities. When we heard that the dragon rider estates were being sold off, we couldn't resist coming out here, even though it is a long way from home. I am somewhat of an expert, you see."

"An expert?" Hooked Nose snorted, as if he couldn't believe a woman like me would have any interest in antiques. He dug out a box from his pocket and popped it open to reveal a heavy gold signet ring. "I just bought this. It's supposed to be the signet ring for House Yanorin, close to two-thousand-years old."

I held back a snort of my own--my treasure sense barely made a peep, which told me this ring was a cheap knockoff. Still, I made a great show of taking the ring and inspecting it for a minute. "It's a fake," I pronounced.

"A fake?" The soldier scowled. "I bought this from a reputable dealer!"

"It's a fake," I repeated and scored the side of the ring with my finger. The gold flaked away, revealing copper beneath. "Real signet rings are solid gold. Not to mention that the design of the seal itself is not quite accurate." I knew all the house emblems like the back of my hand.

"Unbelievable." Hooked Nose took the ring back, shaking his head. "Well, it seems you are who you say you are. I'll be having a talk with that dealer."

"You should go to the Treasure Trove next time you're looking for antiques," I suggested, inwardly getting a kick out of sending the enemy to my own shop.

"Isn't that in the Lower City?" Strawberry Blond asked. "They don't sell high-quality items like that down there."

"My husband and I stopped by there earlier today, and we found the shop to be surprisingly well-stocked with valuable items." I tried not to bristle at the insult. It would seem that our location would always work against us, no matter how good of a reputation we'd built up. "If you are a collector, I would recommend a visit."

"I'll keep that in mind." Hooked Nose inclined his head. "Thank you for your time, Mrs. Brighton."

The two soldiers left, and I locked the door behind them, though I knew it was no use. I was sure I'd locked it before and they'd entered--they must have a master key that gave them access to all the rooms. I imagined that these searches and inter-rogations put a damper on the guests' experience, but I hadn't heard anyone complain about it over lunch, so they must not mind too much. I wouldn't be surprised if the hotel had been stolen from the original proprietor and given to a collaborator, someone who wouldn't mind giving Zallabarian soldiers free run of the place.

Wired from the exchange, I went to the bar to pour myself a drink, then settled in a chair by the window with a book, hoping the wine and the story would allow me to relax. But an hour later, someone knocked on the door again.

"Who is it?" I called, a little exasperated. What was the point of renting a private suite if people were going to bug you anyway? I might as well have camped out in the lobby instead.

"Sergeant Hickley," a man called back. After a moment, he added. "The one with the phony signet ring."

"Oh." *Hooked Nose.* Frowning, I set the book aside and went to answer the door, my stomach tightening with nerves. Why was he back? Did something about my story or behavior set him off? Palming a dagger, I slid it up the sleeve of my left hand, loosely cradling the tip in my palm just in case I needed to use it.

"Sorry to bother you again, ma'am," the sergeant said when I opened the door, "but I require your services."

"My services?" I stared at him, non-plussed.

"As an antiquities expert. I have some more items I need

verified, quite important ones, actually. You will be compensated for your time."

"I see." It was on the tip of my tongue to refuse, but I didn't want to arouse his suspicions. A legitimate trader wouldn't balk at any business opportunity. Besides, making friends with him might prove useful. "I will help if I can. When does this need to be done?"

"Preferably now."

"Very well. Give me a minute to make myself presentable."

I changed back into my day dress, then left Tavarian a quick note explaining where I was going. The sergeant took me to a house a few blocks away, where I was shown into what had once been a parlor room, judging by the sideboard and the pretty pink-and-white striped wallpaper. My treasure sense went nuts as we approached several long tables that had been arranged in rows, and I hid a wince as I muted the sound, which was like a cacophony of bells clanging in my head. There was a fortune's worth of relics and valuables here.

"Where did you find these?" I breathed, picking up a priceless vase. The ceramic gleamed softly in the light streaming in through the windows, and I admired the painstakingly detailed floral designs painted onto it. "This is Golden Age. Worth at least fifty gold dorans."

"Really?" The sergeant seemed pleased. "I'm glad to hear that. We confiscated these from a dragon rider's estate. Most of them will be sent back home to Zallabar, to be displayed in museums, but my fellow officers and I would like to present a few of the most valuable ones to the autocrator. A sort of souvenir to commemorate this visit, if you will."

"I see." My stomach turned sour at the thought of the autocrator getting his hands on any of these, and I was appalled at the idea of our relics being displayed in foreign museums, as if our country had already been relegated to the annals of history. But I hid those thoughts behind a bright smile and said, "I'd be more than happy to assist."

The sergeant wanted me to verify that everything on the tables was genuine, so I spent the next two hours painstakingly studying each object, even though my treasure sense told me in an instant which items were most valuable. Part of me was tempted to declare some of the pricier pieces as fakes, but I didn't want to push my luck just now. I didn't need that coming back to bite me later if the sergeant used a second person to verify them.

"I think you should hand him these," I said when I was finished, pointing to three items I'd set aside: the Golden Age vase, a broadsword with a golden hilt that was studded with gems set into the shape of the family's sigil, and a painting of a dragon and a sea monster fighting on the open sea. The last one especially pained me to walk away from; I would have loved to hang it up in the shop. I wondered what the autocrator would do with it. Would he proudly display this obvious depiction of dragon strength? And how would the others react to it? I knew very well from the rescue mission I'd undertaken to free our captured dragons that the Zallabarians were split on this issue: some supported the autocrator's plan to harness the dragons for his own use, while others thought they should all be slaughtered.

"Yes," the sergeant agreed, admiring each piece in turn. His eyes were shining when he finally turned back to me. "Excellent work, Mrs. Brighton. Your fee, as promised."

He handed me a small gold purse, and judging by the weight, I suspected he'd given me a bonus. "When do you think you'll be presenting these to the autocrator?" I asked, tucking the pouch into one of my skirt pockets. "I would love to be there when he receives them."

"Oh, I won't be presenting them personally." The sergeant blushed. "My captain will have that honor, at the reception."

"Reception?" I tried not to sound too excited. "I didn't realize there was going to be one. Is there a way for me to get an invitation?"

The sergeant winced. "I'm afraid I've said too much already. The fact that there even *is* a reception is supposed to be a secret, and only the highest officials and officers will be invited, so you won't be able to attend. But," he added in a cheerful voice, "I will tell my captain all about your work. It is much appreciated."

"Thank you." I was a little disappointed, but this was still a great lead. If we could find out where the reception was, we could sneak in and try to take out the autocrator there.

I walked back to the hotel, the coin purse feeling heftier in my skirts than it should. I had mixed feelings about helping the sergeant, and especially about profiting off pilfered Elantian goods. Yet the sergeant had given me valuable intel, even if he'd done so unwittingly. Maybe I would find a way to get the coin to those who'd been displaced by the invasion instead. That way this Zallabarian blood money could at least go to a good cause.

I returned to the suite to find Tavarian seated at the dining table, waiting for me. "Ah, there you are," he said. He got up to embrace me, and then led me over to the table. A small feast was laid out: garlic roasted chicken, new potatoes, asparagus, hot buttered rolls, and chocolate cake. "I was hoping you'd be back in time for dinner."

"Didn't feel like eating out?" I sat down next to him, my mouth watering at the sight of the food.

"Skies no." He picked up a carving knife and began cutting up the chicken. "I've had enough of people today."

I laughed, understanding the feeling very well. The worst thing about living at the base on Polyba was the utter lack of solitude. As a treasure hunter and scholar, I was used to spending long periods alone, either shut up in my apartment studying old tomes and maps or trekking in the wilderness. I liked spending time with people, enjoyed talking and laughing and eating together with them, but when I was done, I was done. And the only people I wanted to be with afterward were my loved ones.

The two of us piled our plates high with food, then spent the next ten minutes quietly stuffing ourselves. "So," I said, leaning back in my chair, a buttered roll in my hand. I was mostly sated now, at the nibbling stage of the meal. "What did you learn today?"

"Not much," Tavarian said ruefully. "Despite frequenting quite a few pubs and shops, I couldn't find any concrete information on when the autocrator is arriving or where he is staying. In fact, I've heard about five conflicting accounts, which tells me that false information has been spread deliberately."

I nodded. "I don't blame them for being careful. The sergeant I helped today was very secretive too, but he did tell me that the governor is hosting a reception for the autocrator when he arrives."

"Is he now?" Tavarian's eyes lit up. "Did he tell you when or where?"

I shook my head. "He regretted mentioning it at all, but it's got to be somewhere up here in the Upper City. We could try scouting out the most likely places."

"There are four off the top of my head that we could investigate," Tavarian said. "But we may not have to. I ran across a member of the Resistance today and gave him the password. He says there is a meeting with the local leadership at eight o'clock tonight, and he's urged us to come. Apparently he has important information to convey, though he wouldn't say what in public. I'm hoping it has to do with the autocrator's reception."

"That's great!" I grinned and reached for the wine bottle to pour myself a drink. I'd only intended to have one glass, but after hearing such good news I felt like I deserved another. Things were finally starting to look up for us...though of course, we still had to pin down lots of details to get this right.

"Even if we do manage to discover the location of the reception," I said, swirling the wine in my glass, "how are we actually getting in? Sergeant Hickley made it clear there was a very restricted guest list, so we can't just buy our way into the reception."

"Our best chance is to disguise ourselves as Zallabarians," Tavarian said. "Someone important enough to merit an audience or receive an invitation."

"Perhaps one of the officers?" I suggested, thinking of the officers I'd overheard at lunch. If they were both on the autocrator's protection detail, perhaps we could impersonate them. If we could find them and incapacitate them in time, that is.

"No, that's too risky," Tavarian said. "The officers will know each other too well—they'll speak of things we're ignorant of, and if we slip up, they'll catch us. We'll need to find out who is on the guest list, preferably a couple, and impersonate them instead."

"There will definitely be high-level collaborators on the list. The trouble is narrowing down who."

Needing to stay occupied while we bided our time until the meeting, Tavarian and I went down to the bar to do more eavesdropping. As we sat at the bar, slowly sipping wine, Tavarian cast the hearing-enhancement spell, allowing us to eavesdrop on a pair of officers sitting at a small table just ten feet away.

"I don't know what the governor is thinking, hosting such reception like this," one of them seethed. "There are over two hundred people on the guest list! It'll be far too easy for the rebels to slip one of their own in. Or even a double agent!"

I surreptitiously nudged Tavarian with my foot, tilting my head ever so slightly toward the two officers.

"Relax, Holland," the other officer said. "We have two whole days to secure the venue. Besides, we'll be searching every guest thoroughly for weapons and magical artifacts. No one will come through the doors armed."

Tavarian and I exchanged a look, and I hid a smirk. Tavarian himself was the weapon in this case, and I doubted anyone would think twice about my little perfume bottle. I'd mixed the poison with a couple drops of real perfume, so that anyone who took a sniff would smell the fragrance. Though, of course, the guard sniffing would soon drop dead, so perhaps bringing the bottle wasn't a good idea. Maybe I should leave it at the suite...

We eavesdropped for another hour, but the officers didn't mention any other useful details about the reception. Still, what we'd heard was worth it: the reception was two nights away! Our chance was coming soon, which meant we needed to find a couple to impersonate right away.

"We should leave," Tavarian said under his breath as he paid our bill. "We need to change disguises so we can attend the meeting."

Right. I slipped off my barstool and hooked my arm through his, and we headed for the lobby. We'd nearly made it out of the dining room when an officer approached us.

"Mrs. Brighton!" He gave me a million-watt smile as he shook my hand. "My name is Captain Blakely. Sergeant Hickley told me about how you helped us select the souvenir gifts for the autocrator, and I just wanted to tell you how much I appreciate your help. We have many more relics and valuables that still need to be authenticated. I hope you'll be around this week to continue to offer your services."

"I'd be happy to," I said, hiding my dismay. I really didn't want the soldiers to come looking for me—I had work to do!

"Excellent. Is this your husband?" He turned his gaze to Tavarian.

"Yes." I introduced Tavarian under his assumed name. "He doesn't quite have my eye for antiques, but he's very good with the business side of things, so I keep him around." I winked, and both men laughed.

"My wife has had a lust for treasure for as long as I've known her," Tavarian said, putting an arm around me. "She is a very educated woman and knows far more about art and history than a simple businessman like myself. You are in good hands, I assure you."

"Excellent." Blakely pulled a brooch out of his pocket. "I bought this from a shop today for my sweetheart. Can you tell me if it's genuine?"

He handed me the jewel, and a wave of shock rippled through me—I recognized the ruby and gold brooch from the jewelry case in my own shop! "Oh yes, this is definitely authentic," I said, hiding my amusement as I made a show of studying it. "Dragon War Age, at the very least."

"That's what the lady who owned the shop said." Blakely beamed as he tucked the brooch back into his pocket. "I paid ten gold dorans for it, so I'm glad to hear she's an honest woman."

And I'm glad to hear Carina charged a very high price for it, I thought as the officer walked away. Maybe I would stop by the shop and visit after all, if I had time in between all this reconnaissance.

After a quick change of disguises, Tavarian and I slipped out of the hotel and headed down the street, dressed once more in simple clothing. Since we needed to reveal our true identities to the rebels, and we didn't want everyone knowing about the extent of Tavarian's abilities, instead of magic we'd used good old-fashioned wigs and make-up to change our appearances, hiding my telltale curly, red hair and making Tavarian look scruffy and less well-to-do. The meeting was being held in the Lower City, in an underground cellar beneath an old, boarded-up tavern. Thankfully, the Zallabarians had abolished the old edict that required special passes to take the elevators, so we hopped on board and were on the ground in minutes.

"Oi, you!" a guard said as we were walking away. We turned to see him glaring at us. "Curfew is in ten minutes. What are you doing on the street?"

"We're just heading home for the night, sir," Tavarian

assured him. "My wife and I had business at Dragon's Table, and it took us longer than expected."

"It's not Dragon's Table anymore," the guard snapped. "It's the Upper City for now, until the governor decides on a new name."

Crap. Of course they wouldn't want to call it Dragon's Table anymore. What other rules and edicts had gone into effect in the city that we didn't know about? We'd need to learn them soon to make sure we didn't draw undue attention to ourselves.

"Of course." Tavarian held his hands palm up, speaking in a placating tone. "I'm sorry. It's just...we've called it that all our lives. It's taking a bit of getting used to."

"Well, get used to it fast," the guard advised. "Wouldn't want anyone to think you're a rebel sympathizer, would you?"

We hurried off into the dark, sticking to shadowed alleys and ducking behind trash cans to avoid the patrolling guards. Part of me wished that we could run on the rooftops, but I spotted guards on a few of the buildings, rifles in hand, waiting to shoot down any trespassers. Bastards. I glared up at one of them as we crouched behind a wall, waiting for him to turn so we could make a dash for the next block. I wished I had a crossbow on me, so I could shoot him down. As far as I was concerned, the rooftops were my territory, and *he* was tres-passing.

"Soon," Tavarian murmured, following my gaze. He put a hand on my shoulder, squeezing gently. "But for now, let's focus on not getting caught."

It took us thirty minutes longer than I'd anticipated to get to the meeting place, and by the time we arrived I was sweating, mostly from nerves. The boarded-up tavern looked forlorn, and I remembered that it had been a popular dive back when I still lived here. What had happened to it? Had it shut down because of the occupation? Or was it something else?

Tavarian and I went around the back, to the cellar doors set into the ground. I rapped on one of the double doors, and once Tavarian gave the password, it swung open.

"Tiana!" I exclaimed, amazed to recognize an old friend. She and I had grown up at the orphanage together, and she'd resorted to prostitution for a while before finally getting a job with a seamstress.

"Hush!" She pressed a finger to her plump lips, her blue eyes darting about to make sure no one had heard. "Hurry up and come in!" She waved rapidly, and Tavarian and I filed past her.

I stared at Tiana as she closed the doors behind us, noticing how different she looked. Her figure had rounded out, and the sallow, pinched complexion from before had faded, leaving her with a healthy glow. She was still wearing her low-cut dresses, but I caught a glimpse of a dagger strapped to one thigh, peeking out from behind a slit in the dress, and another one tucked up her sleeve. Definitely not the Tiana I'd left behind.

"I'd say you're a sight for sore eyes," she said once she'd shut the doors behind us and locked them from the inside, "but I barely recognize you, Zara."

I laughed, pulling off the wig. "Trust me, I'm still the same old Zara Kenrook."

"No, you're not." She embraced me fondly, enveloping me in the sweet floral perfume she always wore, then pulling back to study my face. "We've both come a long way, haven't we? Me, a rebel, and you, dragon rider and leader of an army. And with a handsome man at your side, too." She winked at Tavarian over my shoulder.

"I guess you could say that," I said, blushing a little. "Where's this meeting at?"

"Just around the corner. Come, I'll take you to the others."

Tiana led us further into the cellar, to a large, rough-hewn round table where a dozen people were seated, deep in conversation. They all rose when they caught sight of us.

"Commandant. Lord Tavarian," Lieutenant Diran greeted us, snapping her hand up in a salute. The others immediately followed her lead.

"Lieutenant." I nodded in greeting, then slowly looked over the others. These weren't soldiers—I could tell that much from their posture—but they were tough-looking men and women, all armed to the teeth, their gazes hard with suspicion despite the Lieutenant's deferential greeting. They were civilians, men and women who'd slipped away from the comfort and safety of their homes to risk their lives for this meeting because they couldn't stand the new regime. But they didn't know me. They weren't *my* men and women.

At least not yet.

After a few questions to verify our identities—asking for information that only the real Zara and Tavarian would know— we all sat down at the table.

"Oron informed us that you're here on a mission," the Lieutenant said, gesturing to a burly man with a cloud of frizzy black hair. He must be the man Tavarian had run across earlier. "That you require information."

"We are," Tavarian confirmed. "Specifically, we are trying to find out who will be attending the autocrator's reception tomorrow night. Do any of you have access to the guest list?"

"No, but it's not that hard to figure out," a blonde with a sharp nose and cupid's bow mouth said. "All the newly wealthy Elantians who've taken over the dragon rider estates will be there, as well as the top government officials. Is there anyone specific you're looking for?"

I resisted the urge to catch Tavarian's eye. We'd agreed not to leak the specific details of our plan in case there were Zallabarian informants among them, but we had to tell them *something*. "We need a married man," Tavarian said, "or at least one who has a regular female companion."

"Ah." The blonde's eyes lit up. "What about Sebur Nole? He's an official from the previous government who threw his lot in with the Zallabarians and is now the treasury secretary."

"Nole?" Tavarian exclaimed. "That's a step up, then, since he was the former secretary's assistant before the war. I knew him fairly well as I had to deal with him regularly." Which meant he'd be easier to impersonate than a total stranger. "But as far as I recall, he's not married."

"Nope, and he still isn't." The blonde wrinkled her nose. "Now that Nole is enjoying his new-found wealth and prestige, he's secured the services of Miyanta Klaii. He takes her everywhere with him and loves to show her off to all his friends and rivals. And, of course, she's admired by the Zallabarians too, since she's inhumanely beautiful."

"Right." Miyanta Klaii was a famous beauty, and one of the most sought-after courtesans in Zuar City. Absolutely everybody knew her, or at least knew of her. The idea of impersonating her wasn't appealing—pulling off her natural sex appeal and ability to wrap men around her finger effortlessly wouldn't be easy for someone like me, who preferred tricking and outwitting my opponents as opposed to seducing them.

"Do you have any idea where the reception is being held?" I asked.

The lieutenant shook her head. "Just a bunch of conflicting rumors. It could be anywhere from city hall to the governor's mansion. I think the guards are spreading false information on purpose."

I sighed—Tavarian had surmised the same thing already. Oh well. Hopefully we would find out from Nole tonight.

"We've given you what you want," a man with thinning brown hair and a scar slashed over his left cheekbone said. "What news do you have for us? When are we finally going to strike back at the Zallabarians? I'm tired of all this sitting around and talking. What about some action?"

"What, you mean stealing supplies and recruiting rebels isn't dangerous enough?" Oron snorted.

"We don't yet have the manpower to strike at the Zallabarians," the Lieutenant said sternly. "That's why we're working so hard to recruit more members. That said," she added, turning toward me, "it would be nice to hear some good news, Commandant."

I nodded. "All I can say is we're making good progress," I

told them. "We annihilated a Zallabarian fleet a few days ago that tried to take Polyba, and we've got units out hitting camps and munitions depots to help weaken the enemy when we make our stand. If our mission succeeds, we'll be able to deal a decisive blow to the enemy. All of you need to be alert and ready to act at any moment." I met each of their gazes. "If all goes according to plan, I expect the tide to turn in our favor very quickly."

Excitement rippled through the room like a live electrical current.

"And what happens after all this?" a curvy woman with killer green eyes demanded. "We can't go back to the way things were before, Commandant. The council members who abandoned us like cowards can't be allowed to take their positions back. They don't deserve it."

"Damn right they don't," a bald man shouted, banging his fist on the table. "They left us without so much as a defense plan and ran off to their vacation homes!"

The other rebels began shouting their objections too, and Tavarian held up a hand to restore order. "Enough!" His authoritative voice briefly quieted them, and he spoke quickly before they could start up again. "I agree with you that we cannot go back to the way things were. We plan to create a new government run by officials who represent *all* Elantians, and not just the dragon riders or the wealthy. We do not wish to make the same mistakes of the past, mistakes that led us here." He gestured to the dim cellar around us.

"We also won't let traitors like Sebur Nole remain in power either, once we take back the country," I said. "Anyone who is willing to sell out their fellow countrymen for a bit of gold isn't fit to lead."

"Hear, hear," the blonde said.

"That's all well and good," the Lieutenant said, "but let's not get ahead of ourselves. First we have to win the war. We can worry about who is going to run the country and how afterward." She turned to Tavarian and me. "Is there anything else you need?"

"No," Tavarian said. "Thank you very much for your help."

We bid the rebels goodbye, then slipped out into the night again. Our work was far from done, and we didn't have a lot of time to implement the next stage of our plan.

Getting back to the Upper City was a pain in the ass. We'd initially planned on staying overnight in the Lower City, since curfew was so strictly enforced, but now that we had a solid plan on whose identities to steal, Tavarian insisted we seek out Nole at once.

Sticking to the shadows, we made our way back to the bottom of the mesa. On our way, we looked for guards to impersonate, but most of them were patrolling in well-lit areas, which made it too risky for us to nab one.

"Hey, Landon," a guard barked. He and his partner were patrolling the street perpendicular to the alley Tavarian and I were hiding in, too far away for us to see but loud enough to hear. "Would you quit your squirming?"

"I can't help it," the other whined. "I had too much ale at dinner. My bladder's about to burst!"

"Well, go take a leak, then! And be quick about it. I don't

need to be explaining to the captain why you aren't at your post if he comes by to check on us!"

The other guard hurried toward our alley, heading straight for the dumpster we were hiding behind. He stopped on the other side of the dumpster and unbuttoned his trousers in preparation to relieve himself.

Tavarian pressed a finger to his lips, and he snuck around behind the man. "Mmmph!" The guard tried to yell out as Tavarian clamped his glowing hand around the man's mouth. He caught him in a vise-like grip, holding the guard against him as the magic did its work, and five seconds later, the man slumped, snoring.

"Landon?" the other guard shouted as Tavarian and I dragged the unconscious man back to the other side of the dumpster, out of sight of the alley. "What the bleeding hell is taking you so long?"

I hurriedly stripped the guard of his weapons and clothes—rifle strapped to his back, pistol and sword hanging at his waist, rumpled uniform complete with fresh ale stains—while Tavarian took care of the second guard, who was coming into the alley to investigate. The guard's clothing was a bit big on me—the legs too long, the shoulders too wide—but Tavarian used his magic to adjust it, and also to match my face and voice to the guard.

"Let's go," he said in a gravelly voice that was identical to the second guard's. He now sported a thick mustache and a narrow face. "Don't forget your new name."

Right. *Landon.*

We approached the elevators, and I gave a friendly nod to

the guards standing outside them. They let us up without incident, but the pair waiting at the top stopped us.

"Private Klein," one said as we stepped off the elevator, sounding surprised. "What are you doing up here? Your shift isn't over yet."

"We've been reassigned," Tavarian said. "Captain's ordered us on security detail at Blakely Hall."

"Ahh." The guard stepped aside. "Yeah, I heard he was ordering extra security there to throw off the rebels. As if the autocrator would stay in a hovel like *that*." He winked. "Make sure to look *extra* vigilant tonight."

Tavarian and I laughed and moved on. Blakely Hall was an upscale venue on Dragon's Table the wealthy often rented out for events, and had been on his list as one of several possible locations for the autocrator to stay in, so we could strike it off now. I wondered if the autocrator was secretly already in the city. If I were in charge of security, I'd have had him land outside, then smuggled him in as a commoner. But then again, maybe he wanted to make a grand entrance. I guessed we'd find out soon enough.

Nole's mansion was on the west side of the Upper City, where most of the dragon rider mansions were located. There were only two guards posted outside, and Tavarian knew the house and the original owners well, so he led us around to a servants' entrance on the side. One twist with my magical lockpick, and we were in.

"Well, at least Nole hasn't sold everything off," Tavarian whispered as we crept through the house. My treasure sense chimed rapidly as we passed room after room filled with priceless furniture and art, and I was forced to dampen it once more so I wouldn't lose my sanity. "The original owners will be happy to hear that, once we win the war and return the house to them."

I smiled inwardly at his optimism, wishing I shared it. It wasn't that I didn't think we would win the war—the chances were slim, but we *did* have a chance—but I doubted Zuar City would come out unscathed. I imagined the collaborators who had so gleefully betrayed their country would rather see these mansions burn than be returned to dragon rider hands. The only saving grace was that at least these weren't ancestral homes —merely the residences the dragon rider families kept in Zuar City. Their family estates were scattered all across the country.

It wasn't hard to find Nole's room; we simply followed the snoring. My spelled boots kept my movements silent, and Tavarian used his magic on the door to make sure the hinges were soundless as we opened it. The master bedroom beyond was cavernous, with a row of windows to the left allowing a flood of moonlight to illuminate the massive canopy bed in the center. Nole was sprawled out on it, flat on his back, the sheets tangled around his legs, and conveniently, Miyanta was there too, curled in against his chest. How she could sleep through that snoring, I had no idea. I doubted she'd hear us approaching even if we'd stomped across the room.

Nole, on the other hand, was a light sleeper. As soon as we approached the bed, he opened his eyes and bolted upright. The moonlight hit his face, illuminating the striking features and the thick, well-groomed beard, and I gasped. "You!" I cried, drawing the guard's sword. It was Red Beard—Salcombe's chief acolyte!

"What is the meaning of this!" Nole shouted, jumping out

of bed. Miyanta squealed as he pulled a gun from beneath his pillow, and Tavarian and I dropped to the ground as he fired three rounds at us. My sword clattered against the floorboards, but I barely heard it over the sound of the explosive gunfire.

"Dammit!" I yelled, rolling behind a dresser to take cover. I yanked a knife from my boot and threw it at Nole, but he dodged with supernatural speed, no doubt enhanced by the dragon-god elixir. I wondered if he still had the piece of heart Salcombe had left with him—I hadn't sensed it anywhere near, but he could have hidden it outside the city.

Tavarian had dropped to the other side of the bed, and he fired a burst of red magic at Nole. Nole managed to dodge, but the blast knocked the gun out of his hand, and Tavarian used the opportunity to rush him, drawing his sword. But Nole was too fast—he spun out of the way and grabbed the pistol strapped to Tavarian's waist. Tavarian dropped the sword, and the two wrestled for the gun.

Dragon's balls! I wanted to join the fray, but with Nole's super speed I'd probably gut Tavarian by accident instead. So I dashed for Miyanta, grabbed her by her long, silky black hair, and dragged her out of bed.

"Stop!" I yelled just as Nole yanked the gun from Tavarian's grip. "Stop, or I'll kill her!"

Nole froze, his barrel trained on Tavarian's chest. I pressed my knife against Miyanta's throat, my other arm wrapped around her naked torso. I had no intention of actually killing her, but Nole didn't need to know that.

"If you kill her, I'll kill him," Nole said in a ragged voice, his bare chest heaving. They were both naked, I dimly realized, and the moonlight hid absolutely nothing. Guess Miyanta had decided to stick around for more than just money.

"You'll miss her more," I lied, digging the knife in a little. Miyanta whimpered as blood trickled down her chest. I imagined a pampered courtesan like her wasn't used to this kind of treatment. Remembering that I was supposed to be a man, I grabbed one of her breasts and added, "Would be a shame to let this all go to waste."

Nole's face reddened, and he swung the gun in my direction. "You let her go!" he shouted.

Tavarian jumped up, grabbed a heavy bowl off the shelf, and hit Nole on the back of his head. He dropped to the ground, eyes rolling into the back of his head as he passed out.

"Beloved!" Miyanta shrieked, struggling against me. "You killed him!"

"He will be fine," Tavarian said. He let his illusion spell fall away as he walked toward Miyanta, and she froze, undoubtedly recognizing him. "Unless, of course, you fail to answer our questions."

"Questions?" Miyanta purred, going soft in my arms. "Why, Lord Tavarian, you know I would do anything you asked. All you need to do is convince your friend here to let me go."

"Let you go?" Tavarian stopped in his tracks, a dazed look coming over his face. I scowled as his pale cheeks flushed—he was staring at Miyanta as if she were a lush oasis and we were standing in an arid desert. "Well, yes, I suppose I—"

"Snap out of it!" I dropped the knife and used my hand to cover Miyanta's eyes. Tavarian blinked, the dazed look in his eyes clearing away. "What the hell, Tavarian!"

"Sorry." He shook his head, looking out of sorts. "She...used some sort of magic on me, I think. How are you doing this?" he demanded of Miyanta.

"Why don't you come closer so I can tell you?" she asked in that sultry voice.

I rolled my eyes and pressed my forearm against her windpipe. "The only thing you're telling us is where your invitations to the autocrator's reception are," I said. "It's either that or you and your boyfriend die."

"Please," she croaked, struggling against me. "I-I'll tell you anything you want. Don't hurt me!"

Tavarian and I tied the two lovers up, though we first bundled them into bathrobes. There was something about interrogating someone while naked that took the gravity out of the situation. It turned out that even if Miyanta didn't say anything, merely looking at Tavarian caused him to sink into a lust-filled stupor, so I found a scarf in the closet and wrapped it around the upper half of her face, leaving her nose and mouth uncovered.

"Skies," Tavarian said, shaking his head as he sat down. "Even like this, the allure is palpable. What kind of sorcery are you using?" he asked Miyanta.

"A gift from the dragon god." Miyanta's lush lips curved into a smile. "He rewards loyalty."

"No kidding." I stared. So Zakyiar could give out more than strength and longevity, huh? Maybe Miyanta had specifically asked for this, since magical sex appeal suited her line of work more than the ability to smash walls or run at super speed. "So you and Nole are both Salcombe's acolytes?"

"We are Zakyiar's to command," Miyanta corrected, her spine stiffening. "Salcombe is merely his chosen mouthpiece. It is the dragon god we serve, no one else."

"How many of you are in the city?" Tavarian demanded. "Where do you meet?"

"Twenty-two," Miyanta said after a moment of hesitation. "We meet in the catacombs still, though we've had to find a different location ever since you discovered us that first time. We are all sworn to kill you on sight. The dragon god will no doubt punish me for failing to do so." She gave a mournful sigh.

"How terrible for you," I said dryly. "What have you all been doing these days? Has Salcombe or the dragon god put you on a mission?"

Miyanta refused to answer at first, but when I pricked her skin with a knife, she was quick to open up. The woman clearly abhorred the idea of her precious body being harmed in any way. "We have no mission right now, other than to observe and report," she babbled. "We are still waiting for Salcombe to return from his trip."

"What trip?"

Miyanta shrugged. "As if I would know. He tells us nothing, which is infuriating, but I can only imagine the dragon god has a purpose for keeping us in the dark."

Huh. Guess Nole didn't have a piece of the dragon god's heart after all.

Nole stirred from his position on the ground. "What are you doing?" he snarled at Miyanta, and then his eyes widened as he saw our real faces. "You!"

"Yes, me. Nice to finally meet you."

"You're going to regret this!" He rolled to his knees and began chanting in a strange language, his face tight with concentration. To my alarm, a black cloud began to coalesce behind him, taking on the shape of a dragon. A feral wind swept through the room, and I reached for my weapon, but my hand trembled and I fumbled the hilt.

"No!" Tavarian cried. He flung out his hands, chanting the death spell, and a blast of magic hit Nole square in the chest. Nole disintegrated, and Miyanta shrieked as she received a face full of ash. A deadly roar shook the room, and a blast of heat scorched my skin as the dragon god vented his wrath at being interrupted. But his nebulous form slowly faded away, taking the wind along with it.

Tavarian sighed, slumping in his chair. "That was too close."

"What happened?" Miyanta cried. "What did you do with Nole?"

"He's dead." I marched over to her, yanked the cloth from her eyes, and grabbed her chin, forcing her to look directly at me. "Tavarian turned him into a cloud of ash. That's what you were choking on just now."

Miyanta burst into tears. "Let me go!" she screamed, struggling at her bonds, but I yanked the cloth over her face and stepped back.

"We have one more question," I said coldly, and she went still. "Do you and Nole have invitations to the autocrator's reception?"

"We do," she said in a small voice.

"Where are they?"

She told us where Nole kept the mail, and Tavarian went to

his study to fetch the invitations. He came back with two envelopes and handed one to me. "It's tomorrow night," he confirmed. "There's no location mentioned, just a date and time."

"How do you know where you're supposed to go?" I asked Miyanta.

"We're supposed to meet at city hall," Miyanta said. "From there, we'll be guided to the real venue. I've been trying to find out where it is, but not even the officers know."

"I believe you," I said. With her ability to wrap men around her finger, they would have told her if they knew. "You've been helpful, Miyanta. For that, we'll let you live."

"Please—" she stared, but Tavarian cut her off, placing his hand against her mouth. He used the same spell on her as he'd used on the guards, and she fell asleep in the chair, her head lolling to the side.

"Let's tuck her away somewhere safe," I told him. "We're going to need her again."

TWELVE

The next morning, Tavarian and I spent several hours practicing our new personas. As expected, Tavarian had little trouble slipping into Nole's smug yet regal persona—if I didn't know better myself, I'd have thought I was talking to the same man we'd killed last night.

I, however, was having a dismal time of it. I'd raided Miyanta's closet—apparently Nole had given her a small one in the adjacent guest room—and put on a slinky black dress and a set of rubies, trying to get into character. Miyanta's figure was a lot curvier than mine, so Tavarian had to use his magic to make it fit. Her hair was a pain to style—unlike mine, it was fine and silky straight, which meant very little volume when I tried to pin it up into any kind of fancy hairdo. I might have to hire a professional for tonight, but for now I settled on a simple high bun and added a flower clip, then used the pots of makeup on the vanity to rouge my lips and dramatically line my dark eyes.

"Perfect," Tavarian said, looking over my shoulder. Our eyes locked in the mirror—well, Nole's eyes, really—and he smiled. "You look just like her."

"But I don't *sound* like her." Miyanta's rough velvet voice came out of my mouth, but in a plaintive tone, not at all like the seductress from last night who'd ensnared Tavarian so easily. I rose from the chair, slipped into a pair of Miyanta's heels, and practiced walking around the room. Miyanta was probably graceful as a swan, but I looked more like a flamingo, minus the back-bending knees. "And I don't move like her, either. People are going to notice."

Tavarian shrugged. "I'll just tell them you're feeling under the weather. Everyone has off days."

I made a face. "That must mean every day is an off day for me."

Tavarian caught my face in his hands, and I felt the magic tingle over my skin as he undid the transformation spell. "Miyanta may be a skilled seductress, but she hasn't outwitted generals, rallied an army, or rescued a fleet of dragons," he said, his silver eyes burning with passion. "I would choose you over her any day."

He kissed me hard, and the spark of frustration inside me ignited into hungry, gnawing passion. Miyanta's gorgeous dress went flying, and the two of us tumbled onto the guest bed together. Any jealousy I might have felt over Tavarian's behavior last night disappeared as he thoroughly made love to me, making my toes curl and my head spin with wave after wave of bliss.

"All right," I panted afterward as we lay together, sweaty and satisfied. "I'm convinced."

Tavarian laughed and pinched my bottom. "Good. Now let's get some breakfast."

We went downstairs to the kitchens, where we raided the pantry for cold meats, cheeses, and bread.

"Do you think that we should continue to stay in the mansion?" I asked around a mouthful of ham and cheese. "We can practice until the reception tonight and grill Miyanta on any relevant information about the local politicians and officers we'll be rubbing elbows with."

"That would be a good idea," Tavarian said, "except that our sudden disappearance from the hotel will be viewed as suspicious. At the very least, we need to check out first, then come back here."

After a bit of back and forth, I put on one of Miyanta's more demure dresses—altered to fit thanks to Tavarian's magic—and headed back to the hotel while Tavarian stayed behind in Nole's office. He'd found heaps of treasonous correspondence proving that Nole had conspired with the Zallabarians, and dozens of files going further back showing that he'd been blackmailing the Elantian government all along, even before the war. There was also plenty of information about who Nole was currently working with, which would nicely augment whatever information Miyanta could give us. Tavarian promised to wait until I was back to interrogate her—I didn't want the two of them alone, in case she somehow managed to convince him to take the blindfold off.

Back at the hotel, I went straight to our room, only to find a soldier waiting outside the door. "Morning, ma'am," he said, doffing his cap respectfully. "Sergeant Hickley asked me to come and collect you. He says he has more relics for you to authenticate."

I hesitated. "Is this something that can wait?" I *really* didn't have time for this.

He shook his head. "There's quite a bit to go through. Be best if you come now."

Annoyed, I followed the soldier to the same mansion the sergeant had led me to last time. Hickley was waiting for me, this time in the ballroom rather than the parlor room, and my mouth dropped open as I took in the dozens and dozens of tables all laid out, heaped with looted dragon-rider treasure and valuables.

"Good morning, Mrs. Brighton," the sergeant chirped. There were a half-dozen officers in the room as well, all looking my way eagerly. "Sorry to bother you, but we have more valuables that need authenticating. We have been quite busy gathering all this together, and we'd like to get it evaluated as soon as possible before shipping it home to our families."

"My wife is going to love this set," one officer said, picking up a pair of candlesticks sitting on the table next to him. He ran his fingers over the ornate patterns, utterly unaware that the candlesticks were actually made of brass and relatively worthless.

"And my father will be very impressed when I bring this home," another said, hefting a massive broadsword that looked to be a genuine Dragon War artifact.

As the officers pawed and drooled over the massive collection, anger roiled inside me. Who did these men think they were, coming into our country and unapologetically stealing our heirlooms? It was so obvious they cared nothing for the history of these things—they were just trinkets, spoils of war to hang in their family homes or sell to the highest bidder.

"Are you all right?" Sergeant Hickley asked, his gaze narrowed in suspicion, and I realized that he was staring at my hands, which I'd clenched.

I forced myself to relax and pulled in a deep breath through my nose. "Sergeant," I said, unable to keep some of the annoyance from my tone, "I am glad you think so highly of my skills, and normally I would be happy to help, but this is far too much work for one person alone, and I do have other matters to attend today."

"Which is why you won't be dealing with this alone," a deep voice said from behind me, and I spun around, shock flooding through me.

"Barrigan!" I cried, taking in my old rival and employer. It had been two years since I'd seen him but he looked the same as ever with a shiny bald head, and thick salt-and-pepper beard that partially hid his ruddy complexion. Today he was dressed in a rich sable colored tunic shot through with gold. His tool belt hung beneath the paunch of his substantial belly—Barrigan had a fondness for apple cakes and was a heavy-set man even at his thinnest—and his trademark monocle was perched beneath his right eye.

"Yes, that's me," he said, blinking at me. "Do I know you?"

Dragon's balls. I'd forgotten I wasn't Zara right now. "I—I've heard of you," I said lamely. "My husband visited your shop several times during his previous trips to Zuar City. I'm afraid I haven't had the privilege yet."

"Well, you will have to pay me a visit while you are in town," he said genially, and I seethed inside at the way his eyes twinkled at me. Barrigan was extraordinarily charming and a fantastic salesman—he'd had me fooled for years before he'd finally shown his true colors when I'd decided to leave and start my own shop. The man had harassed Carina and me for years, spreading terrible rumors about our shop and driving away all our customers. As the foremost authority on artifacts and antiques in Zuar City, his word was law, and his lies had nearly been the death sentence of our business.

Seeing no way out of this, I set to work. Barrigan and I spent the next hour cataloging artifacts, starting with the least valuable ones. I was loath to get to the higher ticket items; I didn't want to tell the Zallabarians their true value, but with Barrigan in the room, I couldn't lie.

"Do you think my mother will like this vase?" one of the officers asked another at the end of the table I was working at.

"It is rather pretty," the second one said, stroking the porcelain blue finish and the gold vines trailing around it with his forefinger. "What do you think, Mr. Barrigan?"

"It is a lovely piece indeed but worth only a few coppers," Barrigan said. "Your mother deserves something more valuable. I, however, would be happy to take it off your hands for—"

"Excuse me," I said, putting down the gauntlet I'd been inspecting. "May I see the vase?"

"Of course." I approached, palms out, and the soldier handed it to me.

"Hmm." I made a great show of inspecting the object, tracing the gold vines, turning the vase over in my hands. "I believe this is a Golden Age vase, worth at least eighty gold dorans. My husband has one just like it in his collection." I gave Barrigan a cool stare. "You wouldn't be trying to fleece these soldiers, would you?"

"Well, your husband must be mistaken," Barrigan spluttered, his cheeks reddening with anger and embarrassment. "That vase is only fifty years old, if that. Surely not worth the preposterous sum you propose!"

"What is going on here?" Sergeant Hickley demanded, coming over to see what the commotion was about.

"Mr. Barrigan was just telling me that the vase I wanted to send to my mother is worthless," the soldier from before said. "He offered to buy it from me, but Mrs. Brighton says it's a Golden Age artifact and worth at least eighty dorans."

"It would seem that one of them is lying, then." Sergeant Hickley narrowed his eyes as he looked between us. "But how to tell which?"

I shrugged. "If it truly is worthless, then why do you want it, Barrigan? An antique shop owner as prestigious as you wouldn't bother with paltry trinkets."

"I—I don't want it," Barrigan said, backpedaling. "I merely thought to help this young man out, to give him something for his effort, since the vase isn't worth as much as he thought."

The effort? You mean waltzing into someone else's house and taking their belongings? I fumed inwardly, but kept a smile on my face. "Well, if that's the case, then you wouldn't mind me doing this, would you?"

"*No!*" Barrigan shrieked as I tossed the vase. The soldiers gasped as it flipped through the air, and Barrigan leaped after it.

His big body thudded heavily against the ground as he caught it, mere seconds before it would have smashed to pieces on the marble floor.

"That's odd," I said, pursing my lips. "I thought you said it was worthless."

"Arrest this man for fraud!" Sergeant Hickley roared, and four soldiers sprang into action. They grabbed the struggling man and put him in handcuffs, while Hickley took the vase and handed it back to the soldier who'd recovered it. "Get him out of here. Thirty days in jail should teach him not to cheat my men."

"You can't do this!" Barrigan howled as they dragged him away. "Please, there's been a misunderstanding!"

Sergeant Hickley turned back to me, ignoring Barrigan. "My apologies. I didn't expect the man to create such a scene, never mind lie so blatantly to us. Thank you for catching his 'error' and preventing him from robbing us."

"You're welcome," I said, and this time my smile was genuine. I didn't like helping these soldiers, but if I could make lowlifes like Barrigan suffer, I would gladly put up with them.

THIRTEEN

As it turned out, thwarting Barrigan wasn't the only useful thing I did. As I cataloged the rest of the artifacts—occasionally lying about priceless relics in the hopes that they'd remain here in Elantia rather than be shipped off to who knew where—I overheard some decent intelligence regarding the autocrator's reception. Apparently, the autocrator wouldn't show up until after everyone else had arrived and been checked, which ruled out the idea of trying to ambush him on his way in. The whole area would also be covered by cannons, which meant that Lessie and the others couldn't rush in for a rescue if we needed them.

"Yes, *we could*," Lessie argued as I was leaving the mansion. "*Serpol can use his magic to shield us from attack. In fact, since he can make us invisible, the cannons would never fire on us.*"

"That's not a risk I'm prepared to take," I said sternly. "*Serpol's magic only lasts so long, and besides, we never intended on having any of you fly into the city. How is your recon going, anyway?"*

"Well enough. We are still memorizing the watch schedules and so on—Muza insists we plan our attack out to the letter, even though, between the three of us, we should be able to annihilate the camp in a few minutes. We were going to attack tomorrow night, but now I think we should wait until after you've finished with the autocrator."

"Actually—" I started to say, but a deafening explosion knocked me off my feet. I slammed sideways into an ornate mirror, which shattered into pieces beneath my shoulder. Disoriented, I pushed off the wall, then hissed as one of the larger pieces of the mirror sliced my arm. Smoke billowed into the hallway, coming from the east side of the mansion.

"Death to the Zallabarians!" someone cried, followed by the sounds of clashing swords and screams. The smoke cleared, and I stifled a gasp as I saw a man dressed in fighting leathers cut down a soldier. The Zallabarian went down in a heap, blood spreading rapidly across the floorboards, and I locked eyes with the rebel. His feral expression dissipated, his face going slack with shock. "Commandant?" he gasped.

"Dammit!" I grabbed a handful of my hair, which was now bright red and curly. What the hell? Was the spell faltering because I was bleeding? Panicking, I dashed into a parlor room, my legs pumping as fast as they could go. A window had been left open, and I dove through it without pause, tucking and rolling across the ground and springing up into a crouch.

"Miss!" Someone grabbed me around the shoulders as I sprinted into the street. Ducking my head, I sucker-punched him and kept right on running. I felt a twinge of guilt at leaving him that way; he'd probably just been trying to help. But I couldn't afford to let him see my face.

"Zara!" Lessie cried as I ran through the city. The magical disguise I was wearing kept flickering back and forth, my skin and hair color changing. *"Are you all right? Do I need to come and get you?"*

"Stay away!" I barked. The idea of Lessie flying in for a rescue made me panic even more—with all this commotion and the guards on high alert, I didn't want her anywhere near the city. *"I'll be fine! I just need to get back to Tavarian."*

Lessie growled in frustration, but she kept silent, merely sending me support through the bond. Knowing I couldn't go back to the hotel looking like this, I made a beeline for Nole's mansion. Normally, it would have taken a long time to sneak back undetected in broad daylight, but since the attack had drawn the soldiers away I was able to scale the iron gate and duck into the house without being seen.

I dashed into Nole's study, where Tavarian was sitting behind the desk, nose deep in a thick tome. He sprang to his feet at the sight of me. ""Zara! What happened?" He took me by the shoulders, and magic sparked along his hands. The illusion fell away completely. His silver eyes widened when he saw the gash on my arm. "You're hurt!"

"I went to the hotel to get our things, but one of Sergeant Hickley's men was waiting there for me. He asked me to go authenticate some more relics for him. I was just leaving when a group of rebels attacked."

"And you were hurt in the crossfire." Shaking his head,

Tavarian pulled me over to a chair. My legs shook as I sat down, and now that the adrenaline was wearing off I began to feel lightheaded and woozy.

"Let's get this taken care of." He placed a hand over the torn flesh, closed his eyes, and muttered an incantation. Glowing blue light flowed over my arm, and Tavarian clenched his jaw as the magic knitted skin and muscle back together. Healings always seemed to take something from him—I wondered if he felt the same pain I did, or if it was just the energy drain that was so hard on him.

"There you go." He sighed as he released my arm, which was as good as new.

I slumped back in the chair and closed my eyes. I was still feeling a bit lightheaded—the healing didn't replace the blood I'd lost, after all.

"Did anyone recognize you?"

"A rebel did, but since he's on our side I think it'll be okay."

Tavarian scooped me into his arms, and I opened my eyes as he carried me out of the study and to bed. "Why did the spell falter?" I asked.

"I'm not sure," he admitted. "But I think it's because the magic is bound to your skin. When you were wounded, in essence the spell was 'cut' as well, which is why it was flickering back and forth like that. Now that you're healed, it should work properly once I cast it again." He set me down on the bed and tucked the blankets around me. "No more talking now. Rest."

I slept hard for several hours, and when I awoke, the golden-red rays of sunset were streaming through the bedroom window.

Tavarian was sitting in bed next to me, reading a book, but he closed the volume when I stirred, and turned toward me.

"Are you feeling better?" he asked, running a hand through my hair. His touch was gentle, his silver gaze soft with concern and affection.

"Much." I snuggled into him, wanting to reassure him as much as I needed to reassure myself. "That was a close call today."

"Indeed," he said, his voice tight. He slid his arm around my shoulders and pulled me close to him. "Damn those rebels for planning an attack now, so close to the autocrator's arrival. The Zallabarians will be more paranoid than ever, and the guards will start lashing out at all Elantians, treating visitors like us as enemies. It is a good thing we are going as Nole and Miyanta, or we would never get near the reception."

"Zara!" Lessie's voice cracked through my head like a whip, and I jerked, startled. "You're awake! Did Tavarian heal you? I don't sense your pain anymore."

"Yes. I'm fine." I sent a wave of reassurance and affection through the bond, hating the anxiety I felt on Lessie's end. "You don't need to worry."

Lessie huffed. "Of course I need to worry. You're fragile and human, and I'm not there to protect you. And before you tell me that you managed to survive without me, let me remind you that Elantia wasn't at war back then, and your life was much less exciting."

I sighed. "I wish Serpol and Yalora's spell had worked." I could have gotten much worse than a flesh wound today, and there was a good chance that Tavarian and I would be caught and killed while carrying out the autocrator's assassination. *"I don't want you to die just because I'm a fragile human, Lessie."*

"If we die, it will be in service of our country and because of our heroic deeds, not because you are a fragile human," she pointed out. *"Besides, you've faced a death god and come out alive, so this should be a piece of cake for you."*

I laughed. *"You sure know how to look on the bright side of things."*

"Talking to Lessie?" Tavarian asked, smiling fondly at me.

"Yeah." I slipped out of bed and went to the wardrobe to find something to wear. "I'm going to go out for a bit."

Tavarian frowned. "Where?"

"To the Treasure Trove."

"Ah." Tavarian relaxed. "You want to make your goodbyes to Carina?"

"That's the plan." Bright side or not, I wanted to see Carina one more time in case this was the last chance I got. She would be absolutely pissed if she found out I died here in the city, just a few miles from her, and never even came to say hi.

I changed my clothes, kissed Tavarian goodbye, then headed down to the Lower City, magically disguised once more in my trader persona.

By the time I reached the Treasure Trove, darkness had settled upon the city, and the gas lamps had been lit, casting a warm glow across the cobblestones. The streets were quieter than usual for this hour, citizens hurrying off to their homes, wanting to be well away from the prowling guards before curfew.

I entered the shop, and the bell tingled to announce my entrance.

"We're about to close," Carina said, her back turned to me as she fiddled with a statuette display on one of the shelves. Her long, ink-black hair flowed all the way down to her curvy hips. She was wearing tight green trousers with ornate stitching on the sides and a black blouse tucked in at the high waist, where a utility belt sat that carried her authenticator's tools. I felt a twinge of guilt; authenticating artifacts had always been my job, since I was the one with the treasure sense, but Carina had been forced to take that on too, since I wasn't here.

"Even for co-owners?" I teased.

She spun around, her mouth dropping open. "Who are you?" she asked, her dark eyes glinting with suspicion. I saw her hand go for the knife strapped to her thigh and smiled approvingly. "Wait a minute. Aren't you the trader who's been helping the Zallabarians authenticate dragon-rider artifacts?"

"Only because I don't want to blow my cover," I assured her, holding both my hands up. "Carina, it's me, Zara. Tavarian and I are here in the city on an important mission, and I wanted to see you in case things went wrong."

"Zara?" Carina gaped at me. "But...you look so different! Is this some kind of magic, like the fan Salcombe stole from us?"

I nodded, taking a step toward her. "A spell, courtesy of Tavarian."

"Right. I keep forgetting he's a mage." Carina blew out a breath, but she made no move to take her hand off the knife hilt. "But how do I know you're really Zara? You could be a Zallabarian trying to trick me."

I smirked. "A Zallabarian wouldn't know about the time you went skinny dipping with our guide in the Calamayan jungle while your father was sleeping in his tent. Or about the time you snuck out of the house with me to go to that revel at the Red Dragon and you puked all over that hot bartender. Or—"

"All right, all right!" Carina clapped a hand over my mouth, her cheeks scalding. The two of us dissolved into laughter, and we held onto each other for dear life. "You idiot, Zara," she choked out as our laughter turned to tears. "Why did you come here? Don't you know you're risking your life, even with this disguise?"

"I don't care," I mumbled into her shoulder, squeezing her tight. "You're my best friend, Carina. I couldn't come to Zuar City without checking to make sure you were okay."

Carina locked up the shop, and the two of us went upstairs to my old apartment to have tea and catch up. "I'm glad to see you're alive, but I wish you'd cast off that disguise," Carina said as she set out a platter of cookies on the table. "It's weird to see you wearing someone else's face."

"Sorry," I said, shrugging. "I can't undo it without Tavarian." Unless I wanted to cut myself again, and I wasn't too keen on that idea. "If it makes you feel better, it's weird to be back here in this apartment again." I glanced around. The furnishings were the same, but the pink throw on the couch and the cute little knickknacks scattered around made it feel like someone else's. "I'm guessing Kira is still living here?"

"Yeah. She's out with Brolian right now—she's going to kick herself when she hears you stopped by and she wasn't here. Do you think you could stay the night? She'd love to see you."

I shook my head. "We're carrying out our mission tomorrow, so I have to get back to the Upper City."

Carina made a face. "Which you're not going to tell me anything about?"

"Just that it's dangerous. And that the less you know, the better."

Carina snorted. "Everything you do is dangerous these days," she said as she added two lumps of sugar to her tea.

I took a sip of my own—unsweetened—and closed my eyes, enjoying the way the hot, fragrant liquid flowed over my tongue.

"In fact, I'd be more surprised if you *weren't* here to risk your life. Weren't you out searching for some mythic weapon to help defeat the Zallabarians? Or were you looking for one of the dragon god's pieces of heart? It's hard to keep all of your adventures straight, you know," she said with a crooked smile.

I laughed, and updated her on everything, including the new base on Polyba, our alliance with the Warosians, and my successful trip to Derynnis's Forge. The only thing I left out was the Dragon Archipelago—there was no reason for Carina to know about it, and the fewer who were aware of its existence, the better.

"I can't believe you actually met the god of death and lived to tell the tale," Carina said, shaking her head. "Somebody needs to write a book about your life, Zara. You're becoming a legend."

I grinned "Nobody would believe it. Everyone would assume I was making up tall tales."

"Don't all the warriors of legend do that, though?" Carina

asked, grinning back. "Hell, I'll volunteer once all this is over. It'll be something nice for your grandkids to read."

"Right. Grandkids." The thought that I would survive this war, that I would live long enough to have children and see *them* raise children, seemed like a distant dream. "Did I tell you that Tavarian and I are engaged?"

"Well it's about damn time," Carina said, folding her arms across her chest. "We can both stand up for each other at our weddings, then."

"Huh?" My jaw dropped. "You're getting married, Carina?"

"Well, not yet." She shrugged a little self-consciously. "But I met a guy, and things are really intense between us right now. Probably because of the threat of death hanging over our heads, what with him being a rebel plant and all."

"A rebel plant?" My head was still spinning, but I tried to slow it down to process what she was saying. "Are you talking about one of the soldiers we sent to reinfiltrate?"

Carina nodded. "His name is Branson. He's hot and funny, and whenever he comes over we stay up all night having soul deep conversations and talk about our future. Between all the sex, of course," she added, and I choked on my tea. "But seriously, Zara, I think he's the one."

"That's amazing, Carina. I'm so happy for you." Tears stung at my eyes, and I pulled her into a hug as a renewed determination lit a fire in my belly. To hell with the odds, to hell with dying for my country. Tavarian and I would carry out our mission tomorrow, and we were going to live. I wanted to see Carina get married, and I wanted to tell tall tales of our adventures to our grandchildren.

"There's the Zara I know," Lessie said fondly, and I smiled. There was a bright future ahead for all of us, if we could just survive this, and I'd be damned if I let the Zallabarians steal one more precious second of it.

FOURTEEN

"There," Tavarian said, tucking one last pin into place in my hair. "You look just like her now. No one would suspect you're not Miyanta."

He stepped back to admire his handiwork, while I inspected the elegant up-do in Miyanta's vanity mirror. "Not bad," I admitted, tucking a stray wisp of black hair behind my ear. It was a simple hairstyle to be sure, but I hoped the jeweled pins we'd chosen as accessories, and the stunning blue and gold dress I'd selected from her wardrobe would make up for it. The dress was tight in the torso and thighs, clinging to every curve before flaring out at the knees. It had a deep v-neckline that plunged all the way to my sternum, but was surprisingly narrow, keeping Miyanta's impressive breasts mostly covered while offering a tantalizing glimpse of the flesh between. The narrow straps left her collarbones, shoulders, and swan-like neck on full display, so I'd accessorized with a sapphire studded gold choker, and a set of dangling sapphire earrings to match.

There was absolutely nowhere to hide a weapon even if I'd wanted to risk it, but the bottle of poisonous perfume was tucked into the small golden purse sitting on the vanity table, next to the array of makeup pots I'd been tearing my hair out over.

"Are you sure?" I glanced uncertainly up at Tavarian. We'd decided it was too risky to hire a professional to do my hair and makeup, so I'd spent the last two hours grilling Miyanta on what all the little powders and brushes were for and how to use them. I'd seen high-class courtesans before, so I knew how they looked when they made themselves up, but trying to actually recreate the look was incredibly difficult. I was worried that the black, smoky stuff I'd put around my eyes was a little too smudgy, and that I'd applied too much blush on my cheeks.

"Positive." Tavarian cupped my cheek and tilted my head to the side. He was back in Nole's persona, speaking in his clipped tones, but I could still see the man I loved lurking behind those cold grey eyes. He wiped his thumb across one of my cheekbones—dammit, I knew I'd used too much blush! —then stepped back to kneel at my feet. "Now let's get these shoes on you."

I groaned as Tavarian slipped my feet into the sapphire and gold heels—I hated heels with a passion. But Miyanta would never wear flat soled shoes with a dress like this, so I'd forced myself to practice walking in them, trying to match that graceful glide I'd seen so many women achieve effortlessly.

"Is Miyanta back in the attic?" I asked.

Tavarian nodded. "I put her back to sleep."

"Is that safe?" I wondered aloud, feeling a twinge of worry for the courtesan even though she was an agent for the dragon god. "I mean, will being asleep all the time damage her mind or body in any way?"

"If I kept her asleep for weeks her muscles would atrophy, and she would awake disoriented and confused. But a few days will not do her any harm," Tavarian said. He helped me to my feet, then wrapped a slinky shawl around my shoulders. "You have a good heart, Zara, but do not pity her. She will destroy us if given half the chance."

Tavarian and I headed to City Hall, the agreed-upon meeting place listed in Nole and Miyanta's invitations. Guards were stationed at the entrance, and we were quickly but thoroughly searched for weapons. To my relief, the guards didn't even bother to sniff my perfume vial, and in no time the two of us were milling about in the foyer with close to two hundred guests. There were quite a few Zallabarian officers in dress uniform, with their medals proudly displayed, flirting shamelessly with the glamorous women in the room. As a well-known courtesan, the officers did not hesitate to engage me as well, even though I was already with a man for the evening, and to my embarrassment, I fumbled through what should have been sexy, witty replies.

"Are you all right, Miyanta?" one of the officers asked. A troubled frown creased his handsome face as he studied me, and a cold shiver rippled down my spine. "You seem...distracted, tonight."

"I had a bit of food poisoning yesterday, and I'm afraid I'm not quite recovered, Colonel," I said, smiling apologetically. "Nole offered to stay home with me, dear man that he is—" I hooked my arm through Tavarian's and leaned into him—"but I couldn't bear to miss the autocrator's reception. This is the first time I'll be meeting him, you know."

"Me too," the officer confessed, lowering his voice a little. "I've seen him from afar, of course, but—"

A gunshot rang out through the chamber, followed by a cacophony of shrill screams. Whipping my head around, I reached for a weapon that wasn't there, preparing to square off against the threat. A soldier pointed a smoking pistol at a distinguished looking man in a suit, whose face was slack with shock. The man clutched at his chest, then collapsed, blood pooling rapidly beneath him from what I surmised was a gunshot wound.

"Nooooooo!" the woman next to him shrieked, collapsing to her knees against him. She rocked back and forth on the ground, clutching the bright pink feather boa she wore to her chest like a talisman, heedless of the blood soaking into her dress. "Save him. Someone save him!"

More guards rushed in to clean up the body and haul the wailing woman away. "Let it be known," one of the soldiers said, holding up a blade, "that any man or woman who comes in tonight carrying a weapon of any kind will be shot on sight. No exceptions."

A shiver rippled through the crowd at the menace in the guard's voice, and the guests quickly turned away from the carnage. "Rebel scum!" the officer I'd been speaking to spat as I stared into the dead man's glassy, sightless eyes. Cold fear spiraled through me along with a healthy dose of hot anger— that could have easily been me. Did the Zallabarians really have to kill him, especially like this? "I hope this one serves as an example to the rest of them."

"Oh, it will," Tavarian said in a foreboding voice. If I didn't know better, I would say the frosty anger in his tone was on behalf of the autocrator, and not directed toward the Zallabarians themselves. "Word of this will spread throughout the city by tomorrow. They'll think twice before trying to pull a stunt like this."

"They'd better," the Colonel said, folding his arms. "Between this and the bombing earlier this week, I'm amazed we've continued to be so lenient with them."

A scalding retort burned on the tip of my tongue, but thankfully the guards called for silence before I could lose my temper. "Please form three lines," one of them shouted, his voice echoing through the chamber. Three guards stood at the front of the foyer, indicating where the rest of us should line up. "We will be escorting you to the reception now."

We did as suggested, and the guards led us through a tunnel in the city hall's basement. I gathered that the tunnel was an escape route used for evacuation purposes, normally hidden behind the large storage shelves that had been moved aside. The guards carried torches to illuminate the roughly hewn path, and the flickering lights gave the atmosphere a spooky feeling, making the guests twitter nervously. The women snuggled in a little closer to their men, and I did the same with Tavarian, though inwardly I was rolling my eyes. As if holding onto his arm would do me any good if we were attacked! What was I going to do, throw him in front of me like a meat shield?

"Relax," Tavarian murmured, his lips brushing the top of my ear. "You're looking rather grumpy."

I let out a slow breath, forcing the muscles in my face to loosen. Miyanta would never allow a pinched expression to settle on her face, at least not for longer than a second or two. I already was at a disadvantage since I lacked her magical allure—looking constipated would only make things more difficult for me tonight.

"Do you have any idea where we're going?" I whispered as I leaned into him, pitching my voice beneath the chatter echoing around us. I didn't know Dragon's Table nearly as well as the Lower City, where I'd grown up, but Tavarian had lived and worked here all his life.

He nodded. "This leads to the King's Palace."

Ahh. The King's Palace was an ornate gold and white building that sat in the center of Dragon's Table. Back in the day, Elantia was ruled by a monarchy, and the King's Palace was Elantia's seat of power. These days it was where the council met and where most of the dragon rider's galas and social events were held. Or at least, it had been before Zallabar had taken over. Now, apparently, it was being used to host visiting dictators.

The tunnel opened up into a well-stocked wine cellar, and we were quickly led above ground, into the palace. As expected, the building was dripping with wealth, and my treasure sense went wild as we passed exquisitely detailed paintings, sculptures, and tapestries that were all worth a fortune. Watchful guards were stationed in every hallway, discouraging light fingers, and I counted them under the guise of admiring the décor. At least thirty were visible on the premises, and many more would be nearby on call.

The guards led us into a grand hall lined with soaring columns on both sides. Blue and white marble swirled beneath our feet, golden chandeliers with crystals glittered above our heads, and music from a violin quartet drifted on the air, mingling with the many conversations going on around us. Tavarian was quickly drawn into a discussion about finance with several high officials, and I surreptitiously drifted away, sipping from a fluted glass of champagne as I searched the room for the autocrator. Despite the crowded hall I spotted him quickly—he was holding court in the far corner of the hall, surrounded by guards. I drew closer, studying the situation—it looked like his equerries were bringing guests to speak with him one on one, for very short audiences. A woman in a frothy lavender dress and a towering blonde wig was being led away, while another lady in deep orange was escorted up to meet him. He inclined his head as she curtsied to him, looking distinguished in his military dress uniform, which was embellished with golden braid at the shoulders and far more medals on the breast than on anyone else I'd seen so far. The autocrator had been a general before he'd overthrown the last ruler, and he was obviously proud of the illustrious military career that had allowed him to conquer my country so quickly.

"Damn," I muttered as I turned away, studying the autocrator out of the corner of my eye. He was kept far enough away that Tavarian wouldn't be able to use the death spell without breaking from the crowd and drawing attention to himself. And

I wouldn't be able to sidle up near him and spritz him with the poisonous perfume, either. What to do, what to do?

"Excuse me, Miss Klaii." A hand gently brushed my upper arm, and I turned to see one of the autocrator's equerries standing behind me. My heart rate tripled—had someone seen through my disguise? "The autocrator would like a word with you. Will you come with me?"

"I'd be delighted." I glanced over and met the autocrator's gaze, which was bright with interest. Of course he wanted to meet me—I was reputed to be the sexiest woman in the room, despite my lackluster performance. A part of me was disappointed in this predictably male reaction—when I'd met the autocrator in Zallabar he'd seemed fairly down to earth, a simple, austere man who eschewed fashion and material wealth. But that didn't mean he didn't suffer other weaknesses of the flesh, and besides, who was I to complain? This was my chance to take him out.

"Your Excellency," I said, curtsying to the autocrator. As I did, I slipped the bottle of poison perfume from a fold in my skirt—I'd transferred it there from my purse for easier access after I'd been searched. The glass felt icy against my skin, or was it just that I was cold? A shiver of trepidation worked its way down my spine, and I felt my breath coming faster. There was no way I could pull this off without getting captured and killed, but at least Tavarian would remain out of harm's way. He would live to restore our republic, and Muza and his mate would have the chance to settle down and rear baby dragons. "It is an honor to meet you."

"The pleasure is mine, Miyanta," the autocrator said, and I

nearly toppled over in shock. The voice that came out of his mouth was higher than the autocrator's, and as I straightened up to get a better look, I saw that this man wasn't the autocrator at all. Someone had found a convincing body double—a man of the same size and build who looked like the autocrator from a distance. "I have heard the tales of your legendary beauty, but they all pale in comparison to the reality."

"T-thank you," I stammered, then blushed, hoping the 'autocrator' would just think I was bedazzled by his presence. If I hadn't met the real autocrator in person, I would have never known I was talking to a fake! "You flatter me greatly," I went on, recovering some of Miyanta's air, "but surely you have met many women of great beauty, Your Excellency. I hear you have traveled the globe."

I flirted with the body double for another five minutes before I was finally escorted away, to be replaced by yet another woman. I guessed the fake autocrator didn't usually get to flirt with rich, beautiful women, and he was taking advantage while he could. Did the real autocrator intend to show up at all tonight? Discarding my half-empty champagne glass, I tried to worm my way back to Tavarian so I could warn him. We didn't need to risk our lives over a fake. Maybe we could find some way to slip out of here altogether.

Unfortunately for me, Tavarian was now engaged in a spirited debate with four men of different nationalities. He caught my eye and gave me an apologetic look, indicating that he couldn't break away just yet. Impatient, I stood off to the side and waited for him, scanning the crowd out of habit. A familiar mane of golden brown hair caught my eye, and I did a double take at the bronze-skinned man in the linen suit flirting with a woman by one of the pillars—was that Caor?

I took a step forward, intending to investigate, and a wave of nausea nearly knocked me off my feet. Stumbling, I clapped a hand over my mouth, then barreled toward the ladies room, in the opposite direction of the Caor lookalike. I barely made it inside before vomiting into the toilet, my hands and knees braced on the cool pink marble.

"*Zara?*" Lessie asked, her voice filled with concern. "*Are you all right?*"

"*I don't know,*" I gasped through the bond as I dry heaved into the toilet. Dragon's balls, what had come over me? I didn't *actually* have food poisoning, despite what I'd told that officer earlier, but if he'd seen me sprinting for the ladies' room at least my story would carry more weight now. Was this part of some hallucination? Or did I really see Caor back there? What was he doing at the reception? The only time he appeared was when he wanted to lecture or warn me about something.

"*You need to get out of there,*" Lessie hissed. "*What if that champagne had some kind of poison in it? Maybe the autocrator is planning on killing everyone on the guest list!*"

"Don't be silly," I said as I stood up. "He didn't bring us here to murder everyone. Besides, I'm feeling better already." It was true. The nausea had hit me hard, but it was gone, and so was the dizziness. In fact, I was feeling so much better I was starting to feel a little suspicious.

I walked over to the washstand and grabbed a cloth, then dipped the corner into the water. But as I turned to the mirror, the cloth fell from my hand to plop wetly on the floor. "Dragon's balls!" I swore as I stared at my reflection. I was Zara once more, right down to my curly red hair and pale skin. Even the magic Tavarian had used to alter the dress had been undone—the bosom gaped in a most unseemly way around my much smaller breasts, the fabric was way too loose around my hips, and the skirt puddled on the floor around me, too long for my shorter frame. Even if I somehow managed to hide my hair and face, I couldn't go back out there like this!

Caor chose that moment to pop into the ladies room, still dressed in his linen suit. "You got out of the hall just in time," he said without preamble, his normally fey features set into worried lines. "The real autocrator arrived a few minutes ago, with Salcombe at his side. Apparently he found a rare magical artifact amongst the Elantian loot the Zallabarians had collected that can suppress all magical activity within a half-mile radius. It doesn't affect deities like myself, of course," he added, a little smugly, "but it canceled out that disguise spell Tavarian cast on you. If you hadn't gotten away in the nick of time you would have been exposed."

"Oh no," I breathed as the dawning horror of realization hit me. Tavarian was still out there, completely exposed! Not only would he no longer be able to use the death spell, but his own disguise would have unraveled by now. "I have to help him!"

Caor seized my upper arm before I could dash out the door. "And what are you going to do, exactly?" he demanded. "Salcombe has given your and Tavarian's description to the guards— they will already have arrested him. It seems he has already saved the autocrator from two magical attacks, and gained the man's implicit trust. He goes with the autocrator everywhere now, especially to any place where there is the slightest risk of magical attack, like here. There is no way you can go out there and remain undetected."

"What the hell is he even doing with the autocrator?" I cried, ready to tear my hair out. Dammit, would I ever be free of that infernal man? "Salcombe doesn't care about this war! He just cares about serving the dragon god!"

"Exactly," Caor said dryly, "and since you have removed two pieces of heart from this plane of existence, Salcombe has been forced to seek other avenues to fulfill the dragon god's wishes. I believe he is offering his services to Autocrator Reichstein in exchange for a divine artifact that will help the dragon god manifest in the human realm. I'm not certain if he already has it in his possession or not."

"What?" My heart dropped into Miyanta's heels, which were now two sizes too small for me and pinching my toes. Frustrated, I kicked them off, and they crashed into the wall, the pointed stilettos cracking one of the pretty tiles. "But I thought you said the dragon god would need a whole cult of believers to manifest in our world again!"

"Ordinarily, yes," Caor said. "But the artifact in question is an ancient gem that was given to a human woman long ago by Astiar, the god of dreams, to resurrect her after she'd died. It is not powerful enough to bring the dragon god back entirely, but I fear it can still give his spirit enough of a boost that he will be able to influence our world directly. That is, if the artifact truly is in the autocrator's possession. I am not certain Reichstein actually has it."

I shook my head. "Salcombe wouldn't be helping him unless

he was certain the autocrator had it," I said, pacing the marble floor with my bare feet. "How do you even know about—"

The door swung open, and Caor disappeared as the woman in the lavender dress rushed into the room, eyes bright and cheeks flushed. "Skies above, you'll *never* guess what just happened!" she started to gush, then skidded to a stop. "Wait a minute, you're not Miyanta. Who *are* you? Guards!"

I didn't have time to think—I just reacted. Leaping forward, I slammed my fist into the woman's jaw, and she stumbled into the damaged wall. Her dark eyes fluttered closed, and she slid to the floor in a frothy lavender puddle, already unconscious. Quickly, I divested her of her wig and clothes, and donned them, tossing Miyanta's skimpy dress onto her naked body after I'd shimmied out of it. The lavender dress was a much closer fit to my own figure, if a bit too ostentatious for my tastes, and the wig had been pre-styled into a towering up-do that was more than large enough for me to stuff my hair under. Miyanta's dark makeup looked ludicrous on my pale complexion, but combined with the wig I looked nothing like myself, so I decided to keep it. I dragged the woman into a supply closet just down the hall, praying to any gods that might be listening that she would stay unconscious long enough for me to get out of here.

As I rushed back to the hall, I found a lacy fan tucked into the widow's skirts, so I snapped it open and fanned myself as I entered the room, assessing the crowd from behind it. Thankfully, the fan wasn't necessary—nobody was paying any attention to me at all. They were all focused on the real autocrator, who had finally arrived. The impostor must have slipped away discreetly, as he was nowhere to be seen.

The guest of honor was surrounded by a group of officers, and as Caor had warned. Salcombe hovered protectively at his left side. I was vindictively pleased to see he looked like a frail old man once more—the dragon god must have withdrawn the restorative properties of the elixir he'd been drinking to make himself appear young and healthy again. But my pleasure was short-lived as I caught sight of Tavarian, who was being shackled and trussed up by a pair of the autocrator's trusted dragoons.

"I wish I could say I was surprised," the autocrator said as the guards forced Tavarian to his knees, "but Salcombe warned me that you and your redheaded thief might come here tonight. I didn't think a man of your position would stoop to assassination, but it appears I was wrong. You aren't like those other dragon rider officials who've gone soft and complacent in the lap of luxury, are you, Lord Tavarian? You're a warrior, like me."

"I am nothing like you," Tavarian said as he met the autocrator's gaze. He showed no fear, his expression ice cold despite his tousled hair and flushed cheeks—signs of his exertions from struggling against the guards. He didn't struggle now that he was bound though—Tavarian was all about economy of movement, and would consider it a waste of time. "I fight to save lives, not subjugate them."

"Please." The autocrator waved a hand, which was unadorned aside from a single signet ring. He wore the same outfit as his body double, but the air of command around him was unmistakable, something the other man hadn't been able to replicate. "Your country was falling apart anyway. I simply accelerated the process. Elantia will prosper under my rule now that it is no longer fettered by your antiquated customs and traditions. The age of technology is upon us. It is too bad you will not be around to enjoy it with us."

"Where is Zara?" Salcombe demanded. "You came here with a woman tonight, didn't you? Some well-known courtesan?"

"Sir, he was with Miyanta Klaii," the officer I'd flirted with earlier said, stepping up to address the autocrator. He stiffened when several of the dragoons pointed pistols at him, and held up his hands in a peaceful gesture. "I spoke with her earlier, and she seemed different somehow. Not like herself."

Salcombe nodded. "Probably Zara in disguise, then," he said knowingly. "Your Excellency, I suggest you tell the guards to be on high alert looking for anyone who resembles either Zara or Miyanta. The artifact I recovered should have stripped her disguise, but it's better to be safe than sorry."

"Very well." The autocrator gave the order to one of his dragoons, who went to relay it to the other guards. "Salcombe, Lord Tavarian is a mere dragon rider, is he not? How was he able to change his face, and that of his companion's?"

Salcombe frowned. "He must be working with a mage," he said, and I sighed in relief. I was worried that Salcombe might have discovered that Tavarian himself was half-mage, but that secret was still safe. "Though how he managed to convince a mage to join the resistance is beyond me. They are loners and recluses, the lot of them, not predisposed to working with others. He is a clever one," Salcombe warned the autocrator, "so beware of his silver tongue. I hear he has convinced the Warosians to side with him, even though these rebels are fighting a losing battle." His eyes glittered, and I knew he was baiting Tavarian, trying to get him to reveal information by making him angry. But Tavarian merely stared ahead stoically, refusing to engage, and I blinked back tears as a wave of pride and grief swelled in my chest.

"Interesting." The autocrator studied Tavarian through narrowed eyes. "Take him away, but do not harm him yet. He will be interrogated thoroughly before we execute him."

The guards dragged Tavarian from the room, and I dug my nails into my palms as panic clawed at me. What should I do? Our assassination attempt was ruined—there was no way I could get to the autocrator now, not with Salcombe at his side. Should I follow after Tavarian and see if I could free him before the guards locked him up? What if they ignored the autocrator's orders and shot him anyway?

"Have courage, Zara." Lessie sent a wave of soothing energy down the bond. *"Tavarian is not a useless toff to be easily dispatched. He'll use his magic to get away as soon as he is out of range. You need to focus on getting out of there and away from Salcombe before he sniffs you out."*

"Right." I took several deep breaths to calm myself, thankful for Lessie's influence. She usually was the hot-headed one, but in times like this she centered me, giving me the ability to think in stressful situations. I glanced over at the autocrator, who was now calmly chatting with several high-level guests to allay the alarm buzzing through the room. Salcombe was still by his side, and I studied him out of the corner of my eye, trying to discern where this mysterious artifact was. Had he hidden it in his pocket? I noticed he hadn't bragged about it to Tavarian. The bastard probably knew I was still in the room and didn't want to give me an opening to steal it.

Knowing I couldn't leave before the autocrator retired, at least not without arousing suspicion, I slunk behind some statuary and pretended to admire a huge painting hanging on the wall. Several men came up to talk to me, but I affected a vapid cheerfulness that quickly drove them away. I waited for a good forty-five minutes until the autocrator finally left the room, Salcombe and his guards in tow, then waited another fifteen before making my own exit. I slipped into the hallway, wincing at the loud clacking noise my heels made against the hard floors —I wished I could have worn my boots, but they would have stuck out like a sore thumb paired with Miyanta's fancy dress. I ducked into an alcove and removed the shoes, hooking the straps over my thumb, then crept on silent feet down the hallway, searching for a servants' corridor I could use to get out.

I managed to make it onto the grounds without running into anyone, but I had to dodge two patrols out in the gardens. My voluminous skirts tangled around my legs as I hurried through the grass, and I was forced to gird my loins so I could vault safely over the back gate without getting the fabric caught on the wrought iron posts.

"Oi!" a voice yelled as I landed heavily on the other side. A burst of fear galvanized me into action, and I darted down the hillside, trying to put as much distance between myself and the guard as possible. There was no way I could outrun anyone in the heels, so I tossed them at the feet of a small tree and raced into the winding streets. Luckily the King's Palace was smack dab in the middle of the city, so I didn't have to run very far to find an alley to disappear into. The third door I tried was unlocked, so I slipped into the back of what turned out to be a restaurant kitchen, and nearly ran into a boy carrying a huge stack of plates.

"Sorry," I whispered as I slipped past him and between two narrow shelves that held various cooking instruments. I walked through the double doors leading into the restaurant before the kitchen staff could stop and question me, then calmly walked to the front entrance and into the street. I wished I'd been able to change my clothes, but I would just have to wing it and hope the guards didn't get a good look at me. For all I knew they'd decided I was a stray animal, and had decided not to pursue me at all.

"Get to the mansion," Lessie said urgently as I walked to the corner. "Serpol will meet you there."

"I can't leave," I told her as I flagged down a hansom. I hopped into the back of the two-wheeled carriage and gave the driver directions to Nole's mansion. "I need to rescue Tavarian."

"I know that," Lessie said impatiently, "and we're not going to let you do it alone. Just stop arguing and get to the rooftop, will you?"

"Fine, fine," I grumbled, though secretly I was relieved. Rescuing Tavarian would be much easier with a dragon by my side, and since Serpol could make himself invisible he could fly me around without drawing attention. "But I need to get my weapons."

The carriage ride seemed to take an excruciatingly long time, though in reality it was probably only ten minutes. By the time the driver pulled up to the house I was chomping at the bit to get out, but I forced myself to exit the conveyance and walk up the path to the house in a leisurely manner, not wanting to draw attention to myself. As soon as I was inside, I raced to the bedroom, stripping off my clothes as I went. I changed into a sensible pair of trousers and a blouse, traded out the ridiculous heels for my spelled boots, and strapped my weapons back on. The weight of my dragon blade, tucked into its sheath, felt comforting against my leg, and I realized just how unnerving it had been to walk into the enemy's den unarmed. If not for Caor's timely warning, I would have shared the same fate as Tavarian. No, actually, it would have been worse, for Salcombe would have wanted to draw out my torment, to make me pay for defying him and foiling his plans.

Finished dressing, I stuffed all the belongings I could manage into my pack, then slung it around my shoulders and climbed out the window and onto the mansion roof. I regretted having to leave so many of our things behind, but I couldn't haul all of it up to the roof and onto Serpol's back.

"*Zara,*" Serpol said, and I heard the distant beat of his wings. A powerful gust of wind nearly knocked me off the roof as he landed. "*I'm on the east side.*"

"Yeah, I figured that out," I told him, walking in the direction the wind had come from. I smacked straight into his hide, but he caught me with his foreleg before I could topple over. Chills raced along my arms as I slid a hand along his scales—it was strange, knowing the dragon was there, feeling his hot breath on my skin, but not being able to *see* him.

"I think I'm gonna need a little help getting on," I told him. "I've never mounted an invisible dragon before."

Serpol chuckled, and flapped his wings ever so slightly. The invisibility spell flickered for just a moment, allowing to see his body so I could find the best spot to climb on. He shot into the sky the moment I was situated, high above the silvery clouds where Lessie and Muza were waiting.

"Thank the skies you're all right," Lessie said, nuzzling me gently. I jumped on her back, and a wave of relief swept through me—it felt like we'd been apart for ages, even though it was only a day or two.

"Does Muza know where Tavarian is?" I asked as I stroked the side of Lessie's neck. As a bonded pair, the two of them could sense the other's location, just as Lessie and I could.

Lessie nodded. *"He says he can feel Tavarian heading east. He is alive, but unconscious, so that means someone is transporting him."*

"Really?" My stomach twisted itself into knots of dread. It had been over an hour since Tavarian had been taken away—he should be locked up in prison right now, not on the move. *"How far away is he?"*

"Not very," Lessie said after a few seconds. *"We should be able to catch up with him if we leave now."*

The three of us headed east, staying above the clouds so as

not to be spotted. *"We're only a few hundred yards from Tavarian's position,"* Lessie said as we slowed.

The clouds had thinned, so I peered through them using my goggles to see what was below. *"We're above Briarwood Forest,"* I said. *"You think he's down there somewhere?"*

"Actually, Muza says Tavarian is up here, in the air," Serpol said. *"He must be in an airship."*

Serpol cast invisibility on us, and we ducked below the cloud cover to check it out. Sure enough, a huge airship hovered above the forest. It was painted entirely black, even the balloon, so that it blended seamlessly with the night sky. If not for the flame powering the balloon, we wouldn't have seen it at all.

"What do you want us to do, Zara?" Lessie asked. *"Should we bring down the airship before you try to board it?"*

"No. The chance that Tavarian might get hurt or killed is too high. Besides, someone is bound to notice, and I don't need a patrol sending more ships to blow us to pieces with those shrapnel cannons." I shuddered, remembering the devastating damage those horrible weapons did to dragon wings and hide. *"I need to get on board while it's still in the air and sneak Tavarian off. Serpol, do you know any spells that we can use to incapacitate everyone on board?"*

"I know a sleeping spell," Serpol said. *"If we get closer, I should be able to put those aboard into a slumber."*

"But won't that affect Tavarian too?" Lessie demanded. *"You can't very well lug his body off the ship!"*

"I'm banking on the fact that he's already unconscious to make him immune from the spell's effects," I said. *"Or will the magic just make him fall into a deeper sleep?"* I asked Serpol.

"In theory it should pass over him," Serpol said, *"but I do not know for sure. You must be prepared for the worst."*

Decided, the three of us took off toward the ship, counting on the night to give us cover. The moon was only a slim crescent in the sky, which meant we would be less visible than usual. The only real risk was slamming into the ship, since it too was barely visible in the night.

When we were about fifty yards away, the dragons stopped, and Serpol flapped his wings harder, sending magical dust floating toward the ship. Several minutes passed, and then he said, *"They should be asleep now."*

"Okay. Here goes nothing." Lessie swooped directly over the ship, and I dropped into the crow's nest, just below the balloon and the searing heat of its pilot light. Slipping on my goggles, I surveyed the decks, looking for any sign of patrols, and breathed a sigh of relief at the sight of a dozen or so men slumped onto the ground in various positions of slumber. I'd been worried that Salcombe might have come aboard and brought that infernal artifact with him, but there was nothing to fear. For once, I seemed to be ahead of him.

Satisfied that the danger was minimal, I climbed down the mast and wandered around the ship, looking for Tavarian. The aircraft was luxurious, expensively furnished and bedecked with Zallabarian flags and coat of arms in every spot. Certainly no mere prison ship, and I guessed that this was the autocrator's personal conveyance. He'd probably landed here, then taken a smaller aircraft to Dragon's Table. But where was he now? Was he planning to come back to the ship, or was he spending the night at the King's Palace?

"Lessie," I asked as I moved down the main hallway on the first level, "Can Muza help guide me in the right direction? This ship is enormous—it could take me all night to find Tavarian."

"Yes," Lessie said after a protracted silence. "He will fly around the ship and help pinpoint Tavarian's location."

I spent the next fifteen minutes following directions from Muza and Lessie as they tried to lead me to Tavarian. In theory it was a good idea—Muza could sense where Tavarian was in the ship, and Lessie could see where I was thanks to our bond—but Muza couldn't see the internal obstacles, and I took several wrong turns before finally getting on the right track.

"Okay, make a left here," Lessie was saying, "and then a right at the—"

Her voice cut off abruptly, leaving a deafening silence in the bond. Panic froze my lungs, and I groped frantically for the bond, trying to reestablish the connection. "Lessie!" I screamed, both in my head and aloud. My palms were clammy, my heart hammering in my chest—it wasn't just that I couldn't hear her, I couldn't sense her at all. Which was impossible, because we were bound together. Even when we were too far away to talk via the mental link, I'd always been able to *feel* her.

But the place inside my head where Lessie's consciousness rested was terrifyingly empty. As if someone had carved out her soul and left a gaping hole.

"Serpol, what's happening?" I cried, hoping he would be able to hear me even though I was inside the ship. We didn't have a bond like Lessie and me, but I was hoping he was tuned into my thoughts. "Why isn't Lessie answering?"

"Lessie and Muza flew off without warning," Serpol said, sounding troubled. "They are headed back to Zuar City."

"What?" I braced a hand against the wall, my head spinning. "Why?"

"I don't know, but I expect they are being compelled somehow," Serpol said in a low growl. "I felt a sudden urge to head in the same direction, but I fought off the manipulation. I fear this is the dragon god's work, Zara."

"No." Cold horror spiraled inside me. "No, it can't be him." A vision popped into my head, one of the many nightmares the dragon god had tortured me with during my journey to Derynnis's Forge, of Lessie turning on me, her mind bent to the dragon god's will. I couldn't bear the thought of that coming to pass, of the world eater pitting the two of us against each other after we'd fought so hard to defeat him. "Please, there has to be another explanation."

"We will find out more," Serpol promised, "but you need to get Tavarian off that ship first. Hurry!"

Pushing off the wall, I forced myself to keep running, compartmentalizing my terror for Lessie by shoving it into a mental lockbox so I could deal with it later. I turned left, then a right at the end of the hall and found myself standing in front of a cabin with a special metal hull and three locks in the door. I used my magical lockpick to get the locks open, then burst inside to find a bruised and bloody Tavarian lying unconscious on a cot.

"Dragon's balls," I swore as I pushed aside a lock of matted black hair. His face was pale and streaked with blood, and there was a nasty wound on his scalp that looked like it needed stitches. To my dismay, he didn't react at all when I tried to shake him awake, which told me he'd either been injured very badly, or Serpol had been wrong about the spell only affecting those who were already awake.

Swearing under my breath, I collapsed the cot, then used it as a makeshift litter to drag him through the hallways and onto the upper deck. Along the way I found some twine, and when I made it to the railing I lashed Tavarian's body to mine.

"Are you there?" I called to Serpol.

"In position," he confirmed.

"Okay." I took a deep breath, then jumped off the side of the ship. I landed on Serpol's back ten feet below, miraculously missing the spikes, and grunted loudly as Tavarian's weight slammed me into his hide.

Serpol immediately took off, speeding away from the airship. Every fiber of my being screamed to seek out Lessie, but we needed to assess Tavarian's injuries so we landed several miles away, still in the same forest. It took Serpol nearly thirty minutes to heal him— the terrible-looking head wound was not life-threatening, but a broken rib had perforated his liver, and he was suffering from severe internal bleeding.

"There," Serpol finally said, slumping in exhaustion. Between the invisibility spell, the sleeping spell, and now this healing, he'd used a lot of his energy. "He will be fine, once the sleeping spell wears off."

"Great." I stroked the side of Tavarian's face. The purple bruise on his cheek had not gone away, but he was sleeping more peacefully now, his breathing deep and even, the lines of strain gone from his face. "How long until he wakes up?"

"Another thirty minutes, at least." Serpol lumbered to his feet. "I smell deer nearby, so I will go hunt to replenish my energy. Watch over him while I'm gone."

Alone in the clearing, it only took a few minutes for the gnawing ache in my chest to make itself known again. "Lessie?" I cried through the bond, calling to her repeatedly, but an answer never came. Tears slid down my cheeks, and I trembled at the possibility that I might never hear from her again. Serpol had to be wrong about the dragon god—there must be some other explanation—

"Muza!" Tavarian shot upright, nearly banging his forehead against my chin. He panted, clutching at his chest as if he felt pain there. "I can't feel Muza anymore." He whipped his head around, met my gaze with wild, panicked eyes that made my own anxiety skyrocket. I'd never seen Tavarian look so helpless —not *ever*. "What is going on, Zara?"

"I—" the tears came faster, and I choked on the ball of grief in my throat. "I can't feel Lessie either," I whispered, my vision blurring. "I think they're gone."

"Gone?" Tavarian echoed in disbelief. "They can't be gone. We're still alive, aren't we? Dragon's balls, this must be some terrible dream I'm having." He scraped a hand through his hair, sounding a little dazed. "The last thing I remember is getting kicked repeatedly while on the ground. What happened to me?"

I shook my head, trying to clear it enough to focus on Tavarian's words. "You were taken prisoner by the autocrator's soldiers," I said. "Salcombe was at the reception, with some kind of artifact that nullifies magic. Our disguises were exposed. I managed to make it to the bathroom before anyone saw the change, but you were caught immediately. We found you all banged up on the autocrator's airship, but Serpol healed you and brought you here."

"Serpol?" Tavarian looked around. "Where is he? Can we still communicate with him, at least?"

"Yes. He's out hunting to replenish his strength."

I called to Serpol to let him know Tavarian was awake. He returned promptly, a huge deer in his maw, and ate it in the clearing while we talked over our options. "You really believe this is the dragon god's doing?" Tavarian demanded.

Serpol nodded as he wolfed down an entire deer leg. "I felt his call at the same time Lessie and Muza did," he said as he crunched down on bone and sinew. I suppressed a shudder— even though I was a meat eater itself, it was always a little disturbing watching a dragon eat because of how brutal it was. They ate the entire animal, pelt, hooves and all, and the bones never seemed to get stuck in their throats or cause any digestive issues. "They were unable to resist, and I only managed to do so thanks to the shielding spell my mother and I have been working on for this. Hopefully the other free dragons have been able to resist, too." He swallowed, then hurriedly ate the other haunch. "I heard noises coming from the ship as I flew back here, so I assume Salcombe's artifact must be within range. That is why your man woke up early," Serpol explained to me.

"Dammit," I swore under my breath. The three of us fell silent, and we became aware of other noises—the clop of horse hooves, the rumble of carriages, the distant shouts of human conversation.

"That could be the autocrator himself, returning to the

ship," Tavarian hissed under his breath. He struggled to his feet and stumbled over to Serpol, who had a saddlebag awkwardly tied to his side. Muza and Lessie had most of our supplies, of course, but Serpol had carried some to lighten the load. "I need a weapon," he muttered, rummaging through the bag.

"Tavarian." I took him by the arm and gently turned him to face me. "You're in no condition to be wielding any kind of weapon. You look like you're going to collapse."

Tavarian wiped at the sheen of sweat on his forehead. "I don't care. We need to kill him." But his legs wobbled, and he fell against Serpol's side.

"You're not going to kill him if you fall straight into some-one's sword," I scolded, slinging his arm around my shoulders. I helped him over to one of the trees so he could sit, propped up by the sturdy trunk. "Serpol and I will take care of them. You stay here."

I hopped onto Serpol's back before Tavarian could protest, and the two of us took off, heading for the airship again. It felt strange to be riding into battle with another dragon, to not have the comfort and familiarity of the bond I shared with Lessie, but I forced myself to focus rather than dwell on what I'd lost. There would be time enough to figure out what happened to the bond after we'd taken care of the danger.

"Salcombe is definitely in the area," Serpol confirmed as we flew. "I've been unable to cast any sort of spell."

"As long as your fire still works, we won't need any spell," I said.

We were a half-mile from the airship when we spotted a caravan of carriages surrounded by uniformed horseback riders heading up the path. Slipping on my goggles, I zoomed in to see Salcombe riding next to one of the carriages and speaking to someone through the window. Was it the autocrator? And why wasn't he inside with everyone else?

"This is our chance," I told Serpol. "They're exposed now!"

Serpol needed no encouragement. He tucked his wings and dove at full speed toward the caravan, maw opening wide. Even from his back, I could feel the heat building in Serpol's chest, and I grinned fiercely as the soldiers cried out in panic.

But Salcombe did not panic. Instead he met my gaze with an indolent stare. That was the moment I should have warned Serpol something was wrong, but it was too late. The huge dragon crashed against an invisible barrier, bouncing backward and crashing into the ground. I jumped off his back before I could get crushed beneath his bulk, tucking and rolling, and sprang into a crouch just a dozen yards away from the caravan.

"So you are still in the game, Zara," Salcombe said, his thin lips curling into a smirk. He looked as old as ever, like a shriveled up piece of paper ready to blow away, but he sat his horse firmly, and I knew he was stronger than he appeared even if the dragon god had taken away his youthful looks.

"Like I would give up," I spat, drawing my dragon blade. The two blades elongated and I hefted the weapon over my shoulder like a javelin. Would Salcombe's barrier repel it, like it had done with Serpol? Was it worth the risk of possibly losing my most precious weapon?

Salcombe snorted. "No. You are too stupid for that. You could have joined me, but instead you choose to stand on the wrong side of history. It is a shame that none of my teachings seem to have penetrated that thick skull of yours."

"You mean you're disappointed that I didn't turn out to be a cold, evil, selfish bastard like you?"

Serpol chose that moment to lumber to his feet, and the soldiers went still, their expressions wide and fearful. They cowered when the dragon spread his wings wide and let out a thunderous roar that nearly ruptured my eardrums. I clapped my hands over my ears and hurriedly backed up, out of the line of fire in case Serpol decided to attack again.

"What is happening, Salcombe?" the autocrator yelled, poking his head through the window of his carriage. He tried to look angry, but behind his glare I could tell he was just as frightened as the others. "Where did this dragon come from?"

"No need to worry, Your Excellency," Salcombe said, barely sparing the autocrator a glance. His eyes glittered with fascination as he stared up at Serpol, not even remotely afraid of the dragon. "I had always suspected there were some dragons who had escaped the Dragon War, but I never did find their location. Still, they should be as susceptible to Zakyiar's call as all the others were."

Salcombe lifted his arms to the sky and threw back his head. A necklace dangled from his right fist, and I froze as I saw a huge white gemstone hanging from the chain. Was this the artifact Caor had warned about? My old mentor's throat worked as he chanted in the same strange language Nole had used earlier, and the hairs on the back of my neck stood straight on end as I realized what he was trying to do. Panicked, I tried to throw my dragon blade at him, but it bounced off the barrier and I had to drop to the ground to avoid the ricochet.

The sound of beating wings drew my attention upward, and I looked up to see the silhouette of a massive dragon fly overhead, its red eyes leaving glowing streaks in the sky. My blood turned to ice—the dragon was the size of a small city, ten times larger than any I'd ever seen before. A fell wind whipped through the trees as it passed, and a dozen dragons followed in the colossal dragon's wake. My mouth dropped open as I saw Lessie, Muza, and Ykos amongst them.

"Lessie!" I cried, leaping to my feet to race after her. Evil laughter echoed in my head, rooting me to the spot as the dragon god's dark presence swept through my mind.

"*She is mine now, foolish girl*," he said, his deep voice reverberating through my very bones. It was the voice of death, the voice of annihilation, and I fell to my knees as every positive emotion, every bit of hope and love and even anger was stripped from my being. "*All dragons on this world are mine to command. She will never answer to you again.*"

I didn't think the situation could get any worse, until two guards dragged a struggling Tavarian onto the path. "Found him hiding in a clearing about a mile from here, sir," one of the guards said to Salcombe. It occurred to me in the back of my mind that they were reporting directly to him, instead of the autocrator and the captain of the guard. But then again, the autocrator had disappeared back into his carriage, no doubt cowering in the presence of the dragon god. I might have taken pleasure in the fact if we weren't in such a dire situation.

"Good." Salcombe gave me a triumphant look. "Kill him."

SIXTEEN

"No!" I screamed, lunging for Tavarian. The invisible barrier knocked me flat on my ass, and I swore viciously as one of the soldiers holding Tavarian pulled out his pistol. Was this really it? Was this how it was all going to end—with my best friend turned by the enemy, and my lover shot right before my eyes?

"Now hang on a minute!" the autocrator shouted, and the soldier stopped. To my amazement, he actually threw open the carriage door and stepped out, pointing an accusatory finger at Salcombe. "You never told me that you were in league with the dragon god!"

Salcombe stared down his nose at the autocrator. "What does it matter?" he asked. "I have kept my word, have I not, and thwarted the assassination attempts against you?"

"Yes, but the dragon god is a foe to all of humankind!" The autocrator's jerked his head to the sky, where Zakyiar was circling. Unlike the other dragons, he seemed a mere shadow, though an enormous, terrifying one. Caor had said the dragon god could never take corporeal form again, but what did that actually mean since he was flying above us? Was he only able to influence the other dragons? Or could he breathe fire as well?

The autocrator was still arguing with Salcombe when Serpol shot into the sky and proceeded to attack the dragon god. My heart leaped into my throat as I watched him pass straight through Zakyiar, confirming my suspicions that he was non-corporeal. The dragon god roared in anger, and the other dragons converged on Serpol.

Tavarian—who had been hanging limply—chose that moment to burst into action, taking advantage of the soldier's momentary lapse in concentration. He twisted out of the second soldier's grip and shoved him into the first soldier, causing him to misfire his weapon. Soldier number two howled in pain, and more gunshots rang out as Tavarian sprinted away.

"Stop firing!" Salcombe howled as the horses shrilled and reared up, frightened by the noise. Salcombe was thrown from his own horse, and the autocrator's carriage team leaped away, leaving the Zallabarian leader to choke on their dust. I tried to get out of the way, but one of the horses knocked me sideways and I cracked my head against a tree before slumping to the ground.

"Zara!" Tavarian was at my side, tugging me to my feet. My head swam as I tried to hold onto him, but he was yanked away by the soldiers again. As he fought them, I stared up at the sky in a daze, where the dragons were doing battle. Streams of dragon fire streaked across the inky blackness, mingling with the blue and purple magic coming from Serpol's shields. It was a beautiful tapestry of death and darkness, and for a moment, I was transfixed.

"I can't hold them off for much longer, Zara!" Serpol cried in my head. He was leading the dragons across the sky in a merry chase, using his magic to keep them at bay. *"You need to act now!"*

A shadow fell over me, blocking out my view of the dragons. It was Salcombe, with a wicked looking knife in his hand. He looked a bit battered from his fall, but the fact that he was standing at all told me he was still drawing strength from the dragon god.

"Time to put an end to this," he said, his eyes gleaming with bloodlust. There was absolutely no trace left of the man who'd raised me, who'd read me passages from history books at bedtime and filled me with wanderlust and a love for treasure. There was only a deep and terrifying abyss, a yearning for power and wealth that could never truly be sated.

Whatever bond had existed between us was truly gone now.

"Salcombe!" the autocrator barked as Salcombe yanked my head back, exposing my throat. I kept my eyes locked onto his as I fumbled for something, anything in my pouches that would help me fight back.

"What?" Salcombe asked irritably as he pressed the cold blade against my throat. The sharp edge nicked at my skin, and I fought against the urge to squirm as blood trickled down my skin.

"I don't want her killed yet," the autocrator argued. He peered over Salcombe's shoulder at me, his eyes narrowed to slits. "She might have some useful inf—"

My hand closed around the perfume vial, and I swung my arm up and sprayed both of them in the face. The two men screamed and fell back, clawing at their eyes, and I grabbed Salcombe's knife and jumped to my feet, looking wildly around for some form of escape. Tavarian was trussed up once more, guarded by the soldiers who had brought him in, and the others closed ranks around us, pointing their pistols at me.

"Water!" the autocrator screamed. "This is burning my eyes out!"

One of the soldiers rushed over with a water flask, and began flushing the men's eyes. "What did you do to them?" the captain barked at me, looking panicked.

I shrugged. "I sprayed perfume in their eyes. What does it look like?"

"This isn't...perfume..." Salcombe croaked. He was lying on the ground, and he turned his head toward me. My stomach turned at the sight of the bloody sockets where his eyes used to be, at the painful looking bubbles swelling his pasty skin. "It's some kind of poiso--" his words dissolved into gurgles, his throat working to make the sounds.

Guess he wouldn't be calling on the dragon god's power to heal him from *this*.

"What's the antidote?" the captain demanded. He gestured for the other soldiers to seize me, and they did, knocking my knife away with embarrassing ease. Skies, I'd hit my head *hard* on that tree.

"I don't know," I said, which was true enough. I had no idea how to counteract the poison. Tavarian would know, but I refused to meet his eyes, not wanting to draw attention to him.

"Liar!" the captain yanked a knife from his belt and grabbed my left hand. He pressed the blade against my forefinger and glared at me. "Tell me the antidote."

I trembled as the blade cut into my skin. "No."

He snarled, and cut my finger off with one clean slice. I screamed as hot pain bit into me, and stared at my hand in stunned disbelief. Blood gushed from the stump where my finger had once been, running down my hand and over my arm in thick rivulets. "Tell me!" he roared, pressing the knife against my flesh again.

"I don't know!" I shrieked, thrashing against the soldiers holding me. They tightened their grips hard enough to cut off the blood supply in my limbs, but I didn't care. I wasn't going to stand here limply and let this asshole cut me to pieces. I would resist with everything I had left.

"Sir," the soldier who'd been helping the autocrator interrupted, his voice heavy with dread. "Captain...the autocrator...I think he's dead."

The captain dropped my hand, spinning on his heel. "Dead! He can't be dead already!"

But as he knelt beside his leader, I saw the truth. Both Salcombe and Reichstein lay still, their sightless, disfigured heads lolling to the side. The wind shifted, stinging my nostrils with the scent of death, urine, and feces. The captain knelt by the autocrator and checked his pulse, and I knew the moment he realized Reichstein was dead—his entire body stiffened, and his back bowed in grief.

"It's true," the captain said, getting to his feet. He pulled his pistol from his belt and trained it on me. "The autocrator is dead. And so are you."

Right before the captain pulled the trigger, I sagged, turning my body into dead weight and dragging down the surprised soldiers momentarily. The bullet whizzed over my head, barely missing the top of my skull.

"Hold her!" the captain screamed, preparing to fire again. But a deafening roar split the night sky, and we all looked up just in time to see the dragon god writhing in the air. A halo of dark red energy rippled out from the sky, knocking the other dragons back and whipping the clouds into a frenzy. Lightning crackled through the air, and the clouds burst, showering us with a torrential downpour.

"You will pay for this, girl!" the dragon god shrieked. *"You will pay--!"*

He disappeared before he could finish his sentence.

The other dragons, who had been attacking Serpol, stopped fighting. They hovered in the air for a moment, stunned, but another crack of lightning galvanized them. As one, the swarm dove for us, and the soldiers scattered, crying out in panic. Elation soared in my chest as Lessie swooped low, snatching the captain up in her terrifying maw, and she winked at me as she flew past. The soldiers who had been holding me jumped away, then sprinted for the woods as fast as they could.

"Zara!" Tavarian yelled over the din. I could barely see him through the rain, limping toward me, his hands still bound. My boot kicked against a body, and I groped for a weapon. Triumph filled me as my hand closed around the hilt of a knife. I yanked it out of the dead man's belt so I could slice Tavarian's hands free, then slung his arm over my shoulder and helped him away from the carnage.

"You're bleeding," Tavarian said hoarsely, taking my left hand in his. I blinked down at the bloodied stump where my forefinger used to be—in all the commotion I'd forgotten about it. With trembling hands, Tavarian tore a strip of cloth from his shirt and wrapped it around the wound. We both slumped beneath a tree well out of the way, and watched as the dragons finished off the enemy. They didn't appear to need our help—they were having a grand time hunting down the soldiers as if they were game, and anything we tried to do would only get in their way.

Once the dragons were finished, they gathered in a wide circle around us. The rain was still coming down heavily, so Tavarian and I stayed huddled beneath the tree, which provided some shelter. Shivers wracked me, both from the cold and the pain, but I did my best to focus, to try to make sense of what had just happened.

"Thank you for liberating us from the dragon god," an unfa-

miliar voice said in my head, and I jerked upright, startled. *"If you hadn't killed that evil man, we would have been enslaved to Zakyiar forever."*

"You're welcome," I said, scanning the dragons. "Umm, which one of you said that?"

"That was Muza," Lessie said, sounding amused. *"We can speak freely, like Serpol, now that the dragon rider bonds have been dissolved."*

"Was it the dragon god who did this?" Tavarian asked.

Muza nodded his great silver head. *"Salcombe found a divine artifact that he used in combination with the remaining dragon heart pieces to summon Zakyiar in semi-corporeal form. We felt his presence as soon as he appeared in this realm, and seconds later he cut our bonds and bound our wills to his. We were helpless to resist."*

"That's all right, Muza," Tavarian said, giving his dragon a tired smile. "None of this was your fault. I'm just happy you're safe."

As we were talking, two more dragons joined in the clearing —Ykos and Kiethara. "What the hell?" I yelled as they landed heavily on the ground, tongues lolling out as they panted from exhaustion. "What are these two doing here? Aren't they supposed to be with Rhia and Halldor?"

"We were," a clear male voice said, and it took me a second to realize it was Ykos speaking. *"But a strange force compelled us to fly to Zuar City, and by the time it released us we were only a few miles away."*

"What happened to us?" Kiethara demanded, thrashing her

tail. *"Why were we summoned here? And why can't I feel Halldor anymore through the bond?"*

As Serpol began to explain what happened to them, Lessie leaned in to take a good sniff of me. Her molten eyes flared wide with anger and worry as she caught the scent of my blood. *"Your finger!"* she cried. *"What happened?"*

"The captain," I said. "He was trying to get me to give him the antidote to the poison I sprayed in Salcombe and Reichstein's faces." I stared down at the bandage, which was soaking through, and realized I was beginning to feel a bit light-headed. Was the bleeding going to stop soon? I applied more pressure and winced as a bolt of agony rippled through my hand.

"She needs a healing," Lessie insisted, looking at Tavarian. *"Why haven't you healed her?"*

"Because that infernal talisman is still blocking his magic," Serpol said. He jerked his head toward Salcombe's body, which was lying a dozen yards away, trampled into the ground by dragon feet. *"It needs to be removed from the area."*

"I'll do it," Ykos said, flaring his wings out. He bounded over to Salcombe, snatched his dead body up in his claws, then flew away, my old mentor dangling carelessly in his grip. I half-wondered if I should give Salcombe a proper burial, then decided to hell with it. Let Ykos dump him in a watery grave somewhere, or beneath a nameless tree. He didn't deserve to be memorialized, not after everything he'd done.

Tavarian gave a sigh of relief as Ykos disappeared from view. "I can feel my magic returning. Do you happen to have the missing digit, Zara?"

I shook my head. "I don't know where it went. It's probably been crushed at this point, so I'm not sure I'd want it back anyway." I glanced back down at my bleeding hand, then stared at the golden sparks skipping along my skin. "Tavarian...is this you?"

"No." Tavarian took my hand in his and lifted it, his eyes narrowing in examination. The sparks raced across his hand, as if testing him, then turned around and sped back up my arm. I squirmed as they tickled my neck, and then I became aware of a warm sensation in the middle of my torso, like there was a glowing core inside my body. "I...I think the magic is coming from you, Zara."

"What?" The world seemed to tilt sideways, and I clutched at Tavarian with my free arm to stay upright. "No, that's impossible. I don't have magic."

"Aren't all dragon riders descended from mages?" Serpol asked. I blushed, realizing that the rest of the dragons were still there, watching us. *"This could be a side effect of the bond breaking."*

Tavarian's face went slack with shock. "Do you think the other riders have magic as well, now?" he asked Serpol. "I never considered such a possibility, but it does make a certain amount of sense. Now that the magic is no longer being used to cement the bond, it's returning to the rightful owners."

"This is crazy," I said, shaking my head. There had to be another explanation! I tried to summon the sparks again, hoping it had just been a fluke, and I shrieked as my hands lit up like bonfires.

"Hang on there!" Tavarian laughed as I flailed my hands,

then reached out and grabbed my wrists. "Let's save the fireworks for another time, when we can focus on controlling it."

"But I don't know how to make it stop!" I wailed, truly panicking now.

"Just breathe." Tavarian locked eyes with me, grounding me with his intense stare. "Focus on one breath at a time. In and out."

I did as he said, pulling in one shaky breath, then another, then another. Gradually, my breathing evened out, and the glow around my hands dissipated. "Incredible," Tavarian murmured, examining my left hand. The wound had closed completely, leaving fresh pink skin over the once bloody stub. "It appears your magic knew exactly what to do."

"Huh." I stared at my healed hand for a second, then took stock of the rest of my body. I felt sluggish, lethargic, but no longer in pain. I lifted my other hand to touch my head, and found no trace of the wound I'd suffered earlier. "I'd say I'm good as new, but I feel like I could sleep for a week."

"*Using magic is tiring work,*" Serpol pointed out. "*I too, am exhausted. But we will have to table this for another time—our work is not yet done tonight.*"

Right. I sucked in a breath, trying to clear my head. "Are any of you able to contact your riders?" I asked the other dragons.

The dragons shook their heads. "*They are all too far away,*" a female said, her high voice filled with dismay. "*Why is this happening to us? I thought the bond would return since the dragon god is gone, but I can't feel my rider at all!*"

The other dragons expressed similar issues, and I felt a wave of sympathy for them. Even though Lessie was standing right in front of me, the missing link between us was like an ache in my chest. "Is there anything we can do about this, Serpol?" I asked the free dragon. "What about that spell you tried on Lessie and me, to change our bond?"

"Actually, Serpol and I have been discussing the friendship spell," Tavarian said. "I've made a few tweaks to it, and I believe we can successfully implement it now that the old bond has been dissolved. The friendship bond will allow dragons and riders to communicate over distances and sense one another's location, but our lifespans will no longer be connected."

Excitement rippled through the dragons at this prospect. *"Can we do it now?"* Kiethara, Halldor's dragon, asked eagerly. The sound of her sassy voice in my head, which sounded like an older version of Lessie's, made me smile.

"No," Serpol said. *"Both parties must be present and consent, and besides, neither Tavarian or I have the energy right now."*

The rain finally started to let up, and Ykos rejoined us. "What did you do with Salcombe?" I asked him. He'd been gone longer than I thought.

"I dropped his body in a gorge, then stacked a few boulders on top of him for good measure," Ykos said. *"Trust me, Zara, he's dead."*

"Good." A powerful wave of relief swept through me. "What about Reichstein's body? We need to bring it to Dragon's Table, show the others that their leader has been defeated."

"It's still in the same spot he fell in," Muza confirmed. It was so odd to hear his rumbling voice in my head, since I was only

able to communicate with him via Lessie or Tavarian before. He twisted his long neck toward the horizon, which was starting to lighten. *"We should deliver it now."*

"We don't all need to be there for that," Kiethara pointed out. *"What do you want the rest of us to do, Zara?"*

I considered the options. "You guys were in the middle of attacking a munitions depot," I said to Ykos and Kiethara. "Was the mission successful?"

"Yes," Ykos said, *"but Rhia and Halldor are probably worried sick. We were camping out when we heard the dragon god's call, and we left them behind."*

Dragon's balls. "You should go retrieve them, then, and bring them back to Zuar City. The rest of you will join Muza. He and Lessie were going to carry out a similar attack on the base outside Zuar City."

Decided, Tavarian and I rode Serpol and Lessie to Dragon's Table. Dawn's rays were spreading over the horizon, so Serpol used his magic to shield us from view while Lessie carried the autocrator's body in her claws. We swooped over the city's main square, just outside the capitol building, and dropped the autocrator's body. Only a few people were milling about—street cleaners and vendors starting their day, and the guards who had not yet been relieved of the night shift—but they all rushed toward the corpse, which to them would have come out of nowhere.

Satisfied that news of the autocrator's death would spread quickly, we banked right, heading for the military encampment outside the city. An alarm blared as the sentries spotted us, but

Serpol activated his shields again, protecting us from the shrapnel cannons.

The other dragons, seeing that the coast was clear, joined us as we attacked the camp's defenses. We focused on melting down the cannons, and had nearly gotten all of them when Serpol's magic finally failed.

"Get out of here!" Kiethara ordered as four of the dragons closed ranks, shielding Serpol and Lessie. The soldiers had switched to shorter range weapons, shooting at the dragons with their rifles and tossing spears at them. "We can handle this!"

"Are you sure?" I asked, but I knew it was true. A few of the spears had found their marks, tearing through dragon wings, but this only served to make the dragons even angrier, and they retaliated by spewing fire at their assailants. The rifle bullets themselves were of no consequence—the ones that did manage to strike bounced harmlessly off dragon hide.

Plus, I was so tired it was taking every ounce of effort just to stay astride Lessie.

Even without our bond, Lessie seemed to sense my exhaustion. Without another word, she and Serpol banked left, taking Tavarian and me back to the Underground Palace. As we flew past Zuar City again, I caught a glimpse of rebels and soldiers fighting in the streets, no doubt encouraged by the dragon attack. I should have felt happy that the citizens were finally rising up against the enemy, but I could only worry about how my friends were faring. I hoped Carina and all my other friends had barricaded themselves somewhere safe. At least the orphans had been safely evacuated and were far away.

"Maybe we should go down there and try to rescue them—" I started.

"Not a chance," Lessie said. "In your state, Zara, you'll just get yourself killed. Carina would be furious."

I sighed, knowing she was right, and leaned my head against Lessie's warm scales, my eyes sliding closed. When I opened them again, I was back in the underground palace, snuggled up with Tavarian and the dragons. A fire crackled peacefully a few feet away, casting a warm glow over Tavarian's sleeping face, and I brushed my hand against his cheek before falling back asleep.

I didn't know how long I was out, but I woke to the sensation of Lessie nuzzling the top of my head. *"Get up, sleepyhead,"* she said, a whuff of warm breath ruffling my hair. *"Serpol is ready to do the spell."*

"Huh?" I lifted my head, still groggy. "What spell?"

"The friendship binding," Serpol said. He was curled up a few feet away, his bronze scales rippling in the firelight. That the fire was the only source of light told me it must be nightfall—had I slept all day? *"I am refreshed, so I can do it on the two of you now. And if it is successful I can repeat it with the other dragons and riders, if they so wish to be bound."*

"Wow. Okay." I pushed myself up into a sitting position to face Serpol properly. Tavarian sat up too, and threaded his fingers with mine in a silent show of support. "Umm, what do we need to do?"

"Let us return to the surface." Serpol lumbered to his feet. "This is best done in the open air, and under the light of the moon."

The dragons helped us out of the Underground Palace, and Lessie and I stood together in the center of a large clearing, while Tavarian waited off to the side. A crisp, cold wind whipped through the clearing, and I took a deep breath of the fresh air as I lifted my face toward the full moon.

"Since you no longer have the original bond, a blood exchange is required," Serpol told us. "Are you both okay with this?"

I glanced up at Lessie. "Of course I am," she said, thrashing her tail impatiently. "Just tell us what we need to do!"

Serpol gave us instructions, and I used my dragon blade to make a small cut in my palm. Lessie presented one of her right claws to me, upturned, and used a claw from her left foot to slash it open. Dark blood welled from the wound, and I covered it with my hand, letting our blood mingle together.

Serpol nodded approvingly, then began to chant in the same foreign language he and his mother had used last time. A blue glow began to emanate from our joined appendages, and I gasped as Lessie's thoughts and emotions rushed into the empty space where our bond used to be.

"It's working, Zara!" Lessie squealed, and I laughed. Her excitement and joy were infectious. "I can feel you again!"

"I know! Me too!" I wanted to throw my arms around her, but we forced ourselves to wait until Serpol was done. A minute later, he finished chanting, and the blue glow disappeared. I pulled back my hand to see that the cut had healed, and so had Lessie's.

"Hmm." I took the blade and slashed my hand again, ignoring the streak of pain.

"Zara!" Lessie cried. "What are you doing?"

I held up my bleeding hand. "Do you feel that?" I asked.

"Do I..." Lessie narrowed her fiery eyes in thought. "No. No, I don't feel it."

"Excellent." Serpol flashed a toothy grin. "I wouldn't have tested it quite that way, but this is proof that your lifespans are no longer intertwined. You won't feel each other's pain anymore, and if one of you dies, the other will not be affected."

"I didn't doubt that, but thank you for proving it," Lessie said dryly. "Now can someone *please* heal Zara's hand?"

Tavarian stepped in and quickly took care of it. "Now that we are refreshed, we should return to the city," he said. "I am anxious to see how the fighting is going."

We flew back to the capital, expecting to see fighting in the streets. But despite the signs of recent battle—damaged property, dead bodies, smoke rising from recently burned buildings—the city seemed contained. The streets were patrolled by civilians now, with no sign of the Zallabarian soldiers anywhere, and I spotted dragons circling both the higher and lower cities, keeping a lookout and simultaneously discouraging any potential dissenters.

Two of the dragons broke away to meet us, and I started as I recognized Ykos and Kiethara.

"Zara!" Rhia exclaimed as her dragon drew alongside me. She looked a bit worse for the wear, a freshly stitched cut on one cheek and a ring of purple bruises around her neck. Halldor also had bruises, and seemed to be heavily favoring his right arm. "I was wondering when you'd turn up. Are you feeling better?"

"Better than you two must feel. What the hell happened?"

"We were captured by a band of soldiers that survived our attack," Halldor said grimly. "They were torturing us for information when Kiethara and Ykos showed up." He shook his head. "I'm glad you freed them from the dragon god's bond, Zara. The enemy soldiers might have killed us if our dragons hadn't come back to save us."

Kiethara ducked her head. *"I'm sorry we left you like that,"* she said.

Halldor patted the side of her neck. "It's not your fault, Kie," he said. "You couldn't help what you did. I'm just glad you're back with me."

"What's the situation on the ground?" Tavarian asked. "I assume the Zallabarians have been routed?"

Rhia nodded. "They attempted to fight back, but the knowledge that their leader was dead, plus all the dragons attacking the city, was too much. Lieutenant Diran is in command right now. She's routed all the Zallabarian soldiers and officials, as well as the sympathizers, and is awaiting your orders for what to do with them."

"Wow." I let out a low whistle. A lot had changed in such a short time. "Guess I'd better talk to her, then."

The dragons dropped us off at City Hall, where the Lieutenant had set up a base of operations. "Commandant. Lord Tavarian." She greeted us with a salute as we stepped into the office she'd commandeered. "I'm glad to see you're still with us. I heard you were injured by that evil sorcerer."

"Evil sorcerer?" I echoed in confusion.

"Yes. The one who summoned the dragon god." She frowned at my puzzled reaction. "Is he not a sorcerer?"

"I wouldn't call him that, no," I said, then decided not to debate it any further. What did it matter? Salcombe was dead, no matter what anyone called him, and he wasn't coming back. "I hear you've detained the survivors. Who is their leader?"

"A General Trattner," she said. "He says he knows you?"

I bit back a wince. Trattner and I knew each other quite well—I'd befriended him in Traggar under an assumed identity, manipulated him into breaking the Traggaran-Zallabarian alliance, then later on conned my way into his home so I could steal a piece of the dragon god's heart from a Zallabarian official. I supposed it was only a matter of time before he learned who I truly was—he must have seen a wanted poster with my face on it and put two and two together.

"I'd like to speak with him," I said. "Where is he?"

Trattner was being held at the dragon rider academy, along with the rest of the soldiers. The Lieutenant sent for him, and I had him brought into a second office, so Tavarian and I could speak with him in private. Two soldiers ushered him in, and I noticed he'd been stripped of his uniform jacket and medals, his hands bound with manacles. Yet despite this, he held his head high, his spine ramrod straight, and met my gaze without flinching as he was made to sit.

"Zara Kenrook," he said with a faint, bitter smile. "Or is that your real name?"

The jab struck home, but I kept my expression placid. "You know it is. Just as you know why I had to deceive you."

He sighed. "I suppose I have only myself to blame, for letting myself get taken in by a pretty redhead with a sharp mind." He sat a little straighter in his chair. "I know what you are about to say, and it's not necessary. I know that the war was a mistake."

I blinked. "You do?"

"Any man with half a brain could see it," Trattner said impatiently, his eyes flashing. "I am loyal to my country, so I had no choice but to go along with the autocrator's wishes. Now that he is gone, however, my only interest is mitigating the damage now that we have been defeated."

"The damage to who?" Tavarian asked, a challenge in his voice. "To your people, or to ours as well?"

"My people are the priority," Trattner said stiffly. "But of course I mean no harm to yours."

"The way I see it, we're holding a lot of your people prisoner, and you're holding a lot of ours," I said. There were quite a few Elantians still stuck in Zallabarian POW camps, both civilians and soldiers. "There are a lot of other details to work out regarding your surrender, but we can start by trading your people back for ours."

"Right." Trattner cleared his throat. "Though I am the ranking officer in Elantia at the moment, I am not an official representative of my country. I will need to confer with the autocrator's advisors before I can make any decisions."

We argued back and forth for a little while before eventually declaring an armistice. Trattner would travel back to Zallabar, accompanied by Elantian soldiers, to speak to the advisors, while the rest of the soldiers and officials remained here. We would meet again in two weeks, here in Elantia, for peace talks. Finished, I had the soldiers escort Trattner away, then called the lieutenant in to inform her of the new development.

"Tell your men that they are not to mistreat the prisoners under any circumstances," Tavarian said. "I don't want to give the Zallabarians any ammunition for the coming negotiations."

The lieutenant grunted. "The men won't be happy to hear that, after all these weeks of suffering, but I'll let them know. Most of them are civilians, Commandant, so they're not as easy to control."

The next three weeks passed in a blur of activity. Now that Zuar City was retaken and the autocrator toppled from his throne, the dragons returned to their riders. The armistice didn't preclude us from chasing the Zallabarians out of our cities, and the soldiers did so with gleeful abandon, led by Captain Ragorin and backed up by the remaining dragon riders.

Meanwhile, Tavarian and I worked relentlessly on re-establishing the Elantian government. New councilmembers from both the Lower and Upper Cities were elected, and together, we hammered out a constitution that gave equal rights to all taxpayers, irrespective of birth. We also finally conducted the peace talks with the Zallabarians, who formally withdrew their troops from Elantia and renounced any claim on our overseas possessions. We also tried to recover the stolen art and artifacts, but that was an uphill battle since so many soldiers had sent back pieces to their families already. Some of the new councilors were keen on imposing punitive fines as recompense for the war damages on the Zallabarans, but the Zallabarians balked at that. Tavarian argued for moderation, pointing out that their economy had already suffered and such payments would surely create more resentment for the future.

As for the autocrator's demise, the Zallabarians assumed the dragon god and Salcombe were responsible, and we did nothing to disabuse them of that notion. While that meant Tavarian and I would never take credit for that, it also kept a lifelong target off our backs.

Of course, not everything was perfect. Though Serpol had managed to re-establish links between the dragons and their riders via the friendship bond, all the dragon riders were experiencing magical outbursts now. At least once a day I found myself accidentally performing little bits of magic—causing random objects to levitate while I was puzzling out a problem, making a priceless vase explode during a fit of anger, and so on. When we all signed the constitution, I became so excited and overjoyed that a potted plant in the corner of the room shot up four feet, its delicate fronds plastered against the ceiling.

"Well that's a new one," Tavarian said, his eyes twinkling in a rare show of amusement as I cringed. "Don't worry—I can fix that later."

"And what about when she does something that can't be fixed?" another council member demanded, his eyes flashing. He gestured to the other dragon rider council members on the table, Jallis and Rhia amongst them. "Someone needs to be appointed to train these new mages, before someone gets hurt!"

"We are already recruiting experienced mages for this purpose," Rhia said in a placating voice. "Believe me, we want to be able to control our magic as well. But there are not very many trained mages around, so it will take us time to establish a proper program."

"What about the collaborators?" Carina asked. As both a champion for the downtrodden and an influential citizen, she'd been a natural choice as one of the Lower City representatives. "They still need to be tried for treason, and not just for stealing from the dragon riders. A lot of Lower City citizens had homes and businesses stolen from them as well, and they demand restitution."

"Trials are starting in two weeks," Jallis told her. He'd been appointed as the new Justice Secretary, and would be overseeing them. "I know they've been waiting, but tell your constituents to be patient. We've only just finished settling with the Zallabarians, and we are still rebuilding and reorganizing all these departments."

Despite all our squabbling, the one thing everyone agreed on was that it was time for me and Tavarian to finally tie the knot. At first I resisted—there was so much work to do, and the time and money were better spent rebuilding. But the others insisted, and when Rhia and Carina jumped in and began planning the whole affair on their own, I decided to let them run with it.

"Stop feeling so guilty about this," Carina ordered as I stood in my old dormitory room at Dragon Rider Academy, trying not to fidget as Rhia and the stylist primped and prepped me for the big day. "You're allowed to take time off to get married."

"It's not just about the time," I complained as Rhia fussed over my hem. I'd intended to go with a simple gown initially, but Carina and Rhia had vetoed the idea. They'd wanted to stick me in a lavish monstrosity with a twenty-foot train, but I'd put my foot down, and we'd compromised. The dress I chose was elegant and form-fitting, with a sweetheart neckline and a short train. The shoulders and sleeves were made of sheer lace, and that same lace trailed all the way down my back, stitched in the shape of a dragon whose long tail disappeared into the ivory skirt. I'd thought about asking them to use red lace for the dragon, but ultimately decided to let it stand as-is. Dragons would always be part of our country's identity, but they would no longer define us, and this dress would symbolize that.

"Yes, yes, we know." Rhia rolled her eyes as she smoothed out my skirt. "You think it's an inappropriate display of decadence. But the truth is, Zara, that the people need a reason to celebrate after months of turmoil. And what better way to do that than with the union of Elantia's two greatest saviors?"

I cringed a little at that. I hated that Tavarian and I had been put on a pedestal like this—taking the country back had been a team effort, and it didn't feel right to take so much credit. But Tavarian was the unofficial organizer of the new system, and I had spearheaded the war effort, so everyone was always looking to us to lead the way.

A knock saved Carina and Rhia from further protestations. "Zara?" Halldor called. "Can I come in?"

"We don't have time for this—" Carina started impatiently, but Rhia's eyes lit up, and she rushed to the door to let him in. My mouth dropped open as he filed in with an elderly man and middle-aged woman. Both had blue eyes and chins identical to mine, and while the old man's hair was pure white, the woman's was threaded with ginger. "I'd like you to meet someone."

I swallowed hard, my mouth suddenly dry. "Are...are you Halldor's relatives?," I asked.

"My name is Ethedor Savin," the old man said, "and this is

my daughter, Sabina, Halldor's mother. I'm his grandfather...
and yours, too."

I knew it was coming, but the information still rocked me
back on my heels. Carina put an arm around my shoulder for
support. "You...you were my mother's father, then?"

They nodded. "And I was her sister," Sabina said, her eyes
shining with tears. "Her sister, and your aunt, though I never
knew she had a daughter."

"What happened between you?" I asked, desperate to fill in
the gaps of my heritage. "Why did I never know about you?"

"Because your mother eloped," my grandfather said gruffly.
"She fell in love with a young merchant marine, Calton, and
when I refused to approve the match they ran off to start a new
life together."

"Is it true that they died?" Sabina asked, clutching at my
hand with both of hers. "We hired a private investigator to look
for her, but he's never been able to turn up anything. I had
always assumed she and Calton had decided to start a new life
in a different country, but I never thought..."

A lump swelled in my throat at the grief in her eyes. "Oh,
you're ruining your make up!" the stylist cried, fluttering her
hands. She fussed over me, dabbing at the tear tracks on my face
with a wet towel.

My aunt looked even more stricken. "I'm sorry," she said,
backing away. "We shouldn't have come now—"

"But you're here." I batted the stylist away and gestured to
the bed. "Come and sit down. I want to know everything."

So they did, and my family members told me everything
they knew about my mother. She had never paired up with a

dragon, but she'd had a passion for adventure, and had been itching to travel. My father was a handsome young man, and as a merchant marine he traveled extensively. He'd been the perfect man for her—an adventurous soul who had given her a chance to see the world like she'd always wanted.

"It seems sad that despite her dream of traveling, they died in Zuar City, and so young," Halldor remarked. "I wish I could have met her."

"Well now we know where you got your wanderlust from," Carina said fondly, trying to dispel some of the somber mood. The stylist slid a pearl-tipped pin in my hair, nearly finished now. "You obviously take after your mother, especially with the looks."

"You certainly do," my grandfather said, a wistful look in his eyes. A tear slid down his cheek, but quickly disappeared into his thick, snow-white beard. "I wish that I could have found her before she died—while I didn't give her my blessing, I never wanted her to run away, and I always hoped we'd have the chance to reconcile."

"We don't want to make that mistake with you, though," my aunt said, a pleading look on her face. "I feel terrible that you've been without family your whole life, and we would like to make up for it now, if we can."

The stylist finally stepped back, finished. But instead of looking in the mirror, I rose from my chair and took my grandfather and aunt by the hand. "I'm delighted you came," I said, "and I would love to visit your estate after my honeymoon and get to know you better."

"We would love that," my aunt gushed. "Your mother's old

room is intact, and all her old diaries and things are there if you want to see them."

A chance to read my mother's diaries, to learn more about her life? My vision blurred, and I rapidly blinked back tears before I could ruin my make up again.

I invited my relatives to stay for the wedding, and Rhia and Carina showed them out so they could go find their seats. "Are you ready?" Halldor asked, offering me his arm. As my only relative in attendance—or so I'd thought, before my grandfather and aunt showed up—we'd agreed to let him walk me down the aisle.

"Ready as I'll ever be."

Our wedding was a grand affair at Dragon Rider Academy, hosted in the outdoor amphitheater so the dragons could watch from above. Carina and Rhia stood up for me as my brides-maids, and over a hundred people were packed into the chapel-like room, which was usually used for the hatching ceremony where young dragon riders carefully handled dormant eggs, hoping that one would hatch for them. That ceremony would cease to exist, once the newly-freed dragons started laying new eggs—their offspring would hatch naturally, and be raised by their mothers and fathers.

Starting our marriage here was like saying goodbye to an old era, and marking the start of a new age.

Tavarian's eyes shone as I walked up the aisle, and my heart swelled with love. He looked stunningly handsome in his dragon rider uniform. "You look incredible," he whispered as Halldor handed him off to me at the dais.

"So do you." I briefly brushed my hand along the braiding at his shoulder. "Fitting, that you're wearing the same outfit you wore when we first met."

He blinked, startled, but there was no time to say anything more as General Ragorin—formerly captain, and now the highest ranking officer and leader of the Elantian army—began the ceremony. Vows were spoken, rings slid on fingers, tears shed. It was all like a hazy dream, and through most of it, I was half convinced it wasn't real. But when the captain finally gave us permission to kiss, and our lips touched, reality crashed back into me. The sensation of Tavarian's mouth on mine was thrown into sharp relief, as well as the sounds of wild clapping and cheering around us. His strong arms circled me, grounding me, and as I kissed him back, I became aware of the gold band circling my finger.

"We did it." He pulled away, smiling broadly at me.

"Hell yes we did." I grabbed his face with both hands and, to the delight of the crowd, kissed him long and hard again.

The dragons trumpeted loudly above us, and I could feel Lessie's amusement in the bond. *"Get moving, lovebirds,"* Lessie teased. *"You've still got the reception before you get to move on to the honeymoon phase."*

The reception was hosted on the grounds, and was open to the public, though the guards kept a heavily fortified perimeter around Tavarian and me, and vetted anyone who wanted to approach us. The first two hours were a whirlwind of laughing and dancing, of speeches and congratulations, but eventually I became overwhelmed by all the attention. While Tavarian was deep in conversation with Admiral Messei, I slipped off to a secluded bench in the kitchen gardens for some privacy.

Figuring that no one was watching, I kicked off my heels and nudged them beneath the bench, behind my skirts. "Ahhh." I closed my eyes in contentment as my feet sank into the bare grass. This right here was bliss. All I needed was a glass of champagne in my hand.

"Coming right up," Caor said. My eyes popped open to see a fluted glass dangling right in front of me, and I followed the hand holding it all the way up to Caor's head. His eyes twinkled in amusement at the shock on my face. "What, you didn't think I'd miss the big day, did you?"

I snatched the champagne out of his hand and took a long drink. "Please don't tell me you're here to give me bad news," I said once I'd drained the glass. "I don't think I can take any more."

"Of course not. What kind of god do you take me for?" He actually looked offended. "I came to offer my congratulations. And to tell you that you've defeated the dragon god for good. Niaste, the goddess of divination, has looked into the future. She says it'll be another thousand years before Zakyiar has the opportunity to manifest again, and even then it might not happen unless certain events align."

Ugh. Seriously? "Well then that's not a true defeat, is it? How can he come back if a piece of his heart has been destroyed?"

Caor shrugged. "Don't ask me. Niaste isn't known for giving details—she's cryptic even on her best days. But as far as I'm concerned, your best defense against the dragon god's return is to encourage people to begin worshipping us again."

I fought the urge to roll my eyes. "I'm not the proselytizing type. If you guys want the people to start worshipping you, you might want to start performing miracles again. How else are humans going to believe in you if they don't see any evidence of divinity?"

"Hmm." Caor stroked his chin. "You have a point. I will discuss this with the others."

He disappeared, and I shook my head at his antics. *"You know,"* Lessie said, obviously having listened in on the conversation, *"for all their ancient wisdom, the gods seem just as childish and dense as humans are. It's no wonder they're not idolized anymore."*

My lips twitched. *"Don't let Caor hear you say that."* I stood up, intending to seek out Tavarian, but my treasure sense pinged.

"Zara?" Lessie asked as I followed the signal. *"Aren't you going to get your dress dirty?"*

"I'll have Tavarian fix it for me," I said distractedly, my mind focused on the hunt. Or maybe I could fix it without help, if I ever figured out how to control my blasted magic...

Ten minutes later, Tavarian poked his head over the rose-bushes, his brow furrowed. "Zara? What are you doing?"

"Huh?" I glanced up at him—I was on my hands and knees, digging eagerly in the dirt. "Oh, sorry. I was on my way back, but my treasure sense went off, and..." I trailed off at the growing smile on his face, my cheeks heating. "What?"

"Nothing." He walked around the rose bush and knelt in the dirt so he could cup my chin in one hand. "It's just that you're digging up the garden in your wedding dress, tossing propriety aside for the thrill of treasure. It's adorable, and so completely you." He kissed me, a quick peck on the lips that nevertheless heated my blood, then pulled away to study the hole. "How much more digging do we have to do?"

He helped me widen the hole, and after a few minutes, we unearthed an antique jar full of ancient gold coins. "Ohhhh," I gushed as I spilled a few of them into my hand. They sparkled in the sunlight, and I stared at them for a moment, dazzled. As a student I'd had no cause to wander the kitchen gardens, which explained why I'd never found these before. "Carina is going to *love* these!"

"You can give them to her later," Lessie said. I glanced up at the sky to see her and Muza land in the field a hundred yards away, all saddled up. "It's time to leave now."

"Already?" I looked back at the reception, which was still in full swing. "Aren't we supposed to give a speech or something before we leave?"

"If we do that, we'll be here for another hour." Tavarian took the urn from me and dropped it back into the hole, then used magic to tidy up the area. "It's better to sneak off while we can, before someone notices."

"Okay." Glancing over my shoulder, I saw that a few people were already coming toward us. Tavarian took my hand, and I giggled as we sprinted toward the dragons. I was barefoot, with grass stains on my dress, and dirt on my skin, but I didn't care.

"Are you sure you want to go like this?" Lessie asked as I vaulted into the saddle. "You can change if you want—"

"Commandant!" someone shouted, and out of the corner of my eye I saw someone running toward us.

"Nope! Let's go!" I kicked at her side, and the two dragons

shot into the air, leaving our pursuers far behind. I whooped as the wind ripped out all the pins in my hair, leaving it to stream like a wild red banner behind me. Exhilaration rushed through my blood, and I grinned at Tavarian, who was next to me astride Muza.

He grinned back, looking a little sheepish. "It's unlike me to run away like this," he shouted over the wind. "What if they needed something important?"

"Then they'll just have to go to someone else," Lessie huffed. "It's your honeymoon. Don't you think that defeating the dragon god, winning the war, and coming back from the land of the dead has earned us a break?"

We laughed. "You're damn right it does," I said, patting Lessie's neck. Jallis could handle whatever it was, or Rhia, or any of the other people we'd left in charge. We'd accomplished some amazing things together, and when we came back, we would accomplish more. Our work was far from over, and I couldn't wait to see what we would do next.

THE END

Thank you very much for reading Secret of the Dragon! Make sure to join the mailing list so you can be notified of future release dates, and to receive special updates, freebies and give-aways! Sign up at www.jasminewalt.com.

Did you enjoy this book? Please consider leaving a review.

Reviews help us authors sell books so we can afford to write more of them. Writing a review is the best way to ensure that the author writes the next one as it lets them know readers are enjoying their work and want more. Plus, it makes the author feel warm and fuzzy inside, and who doesn't want that? ;)

And if you'd like to read more Jasmine Walt books, turn to the back of this book for a list of her other works!

ABOUT THE AUTHOR

NYT bestseller JASMINE WALT is obsessed with books, chocolate, and sharp objects. Somehow, those three things melded together in her head and transformed into a desire to write, usually fantastical stuff with a healthy dose of action and romance.

Her characters are a little (okay, a lot) on the snarky side, and they swear, but they mean well. Even the villains some-times. When Jasmine isn't chained to her keyboard, you can find her practicing her triangle choke on the mats, spending time with her family, or binge-watching superhero shows. Drop her a line anytime at jasmine@jasminewalt.com, or visit her at www.jasminewalt.com.

Her Dark Protectors

Written under Jada Storm, with Emily Goodwin

Cursed by Night

Kissed by Night

Hidden by Night

Broken by Night

The Dragon's Gift Trilogy

Written under Jada Storm

Dragon's Gift

Dragon's Blood

Dragon's Curse

The Legend of Tariel:

Written as Jada Storm

Kingdom of Storms

Den of Thieves